'I don'  **desired** ....**by flashed pure venom** ....**on th** **detest you.'**

Remy caught a coil of her h....... **ibra**...... d her to him. He watched as her .... ude.... flared and her tongue swe.... .... of .... There was something in........ .... bout her defiant stance. She p...... .... push. She had always stood u.. .. ..enged him. Annoyed him. Go.... d hi

'I'll have you .... y hand soon enough.' He gave he.. .... it smile. 'You won't be able to resist

She grabbed her h.... and ...... d it out of his hold. 'I can't belie.. yo.. ... ...ng so ruthless about this.' She co........ to .....re at him. 'You don't want me at ...... You just want to win the upper hand.

'Oh, I want yo.. ... .rincess,' he drawled. 'Make no mistak.. ....t. And what I want I get. Every. Single.

'Then you've met your match, Remy Caffarelli, because I bend my will to no man. If you want to sleep with me then you'll have to tie me to the bed first.'

Remy smiled a sinful smile. 'I can hardly wait.'

THOSE
SCANDALOUS CAFFARELLIS

Rich. Ruthless. Irresistible.

Brothers Rafe, Raoul and Remy
are better known as the Three Rs:

1. Rich—
Italy's most brilliant billionaires.

2. Ruthless—
they'll do anything to protect their place at the top.

3. Irresistible—
their business prowess is rivalled only by
their reputation in the bedroom.

(Just ask any glittering socialite they've ever met!)

You read Rafe's story in:
NEVER SAY NO TO A CAFFARELLI
September 2013

Last month you read Raoul's story in:
NEVER UNDERESTIMATE A CAFFARELLI
October 2013

This month read Remy's story in:
NEVER GAMBLE WITH A CAFFARELLI
November 2013

NEVER GAMBLE WITH A CAFFARELLI

BY
MELANIE MILBURNE

MILLS & BOON

First published in Great Britain 2013
by Mills & Boon, an imprint of Harlequin (UK) Limited.
Harlequin (UK) Limited, Eton House, 18-24 Paradise Road,
Richmond, Surrey TW9 1SR

© Melanie Milburne 2013

ISBN: 978 0 263 90061 3

Harlequin (UK) policy is to use papers that are natural, renewable and recyclable products and made from wood grown in sustainable forests. The logging and manufacturing process conform to the legal environmental regulations of the country of origin.

Printed and bound in Spain
by Blackprint CPI, Barcelona

From as soon as **Melanie Milburne** could pick up a pen she knew she wanted to write. It was when she picked up her first Mills and Boon® at seventeen that she realised she wanted to write romance. After being distracted for a few years by meeting and marrying her own handsome hero, surgeon husband Steve, and having two boys, plus completing a Masters of Education and becoming a nationally ranked athlete (masters swimming), she decided to write. Five submissions later she sold her first book and is now a multi-published, award-winning *USA TODAY* bestselling author. In 2008 she won the Australian Romance Readers' Association most popular category/series romance, and in 2011 she won the prestigious Romance Writers of Australia R*BY award.

Melanie loves to hear from her readers via her website, www.melaniemilburne.com.au or on Facebook: www.facebook.com/pages/Melanie-Milburne/351594482609.

Recent titles by the same author:

NEVER UNDERESTIMATE A CAFFARELLI
   (Those Scandalous Caffarellis)
NEVER SAY NO TO A CAFFARELLI
   (Those Scandalous Caffarellis)
HIS FINAL BARGAIN
UNCOVERING THE SILVERI SECRET

To my dear friend Heather Last, whom I met on the first day of kindergarten a very long time ago!

Thank you for always being my friend and for being one of the first people to say:

'You should write!'

Much love. xx

CHAPTER ONE

'WHAT DO YOU mean you *lost* it?' Angelique stared at her father in abject horror.

Henri Marchand gave a negligent shrug but she could see his Adam's apple moving up and down as if he'd just had to swallow something unpleasant. But then, losing her late mother's ancestral home in the highlands of Scotland in a poker game in Las Vegas was about as bitter a flavour as you could taste, Angelique supposed.

'I was doing all right until Remy Caffarelli tricked me into thinking he was on a losing streak,' he said. 'We played for hours with him losing just about every hand. I thought I'd clean him up once and for all. I put down my best hand in a winner-takes-all deal but then he went and trumped it.'

Angelique felt her spine turn to ice and her blood heat to boiling. 'Tell me you did *not* lose Tarrantloch to Remy Caffarelli.' He was her worst enemy. The one man she would do anything to avoid—to avoid even thinking about!

'I'll win it back.' Her father spouted the problem gambler's credo with arrogant confidence. 'I'll challenge him to another game. I'll up the stakes. He won't be able to resist another—'

'And lose even *more*?' She threw him an exasperated

look. 'He set you up. Can't you see that? He's always had you in his sights but you made it a hundred times worse, sabotaging his hotel development in Spain. How could you have fallen for such a trick?'

'I'll outsmart him this time. You'll see. He thinks he's so clever but I'll get him back where it *really* hurts.'

Angelique rolled her eyes and turned away. Her stomach felt as if it had been scraped out with a rusty spoon. How could her father have lost her beloved mother's ancestral home to Remy Caffarelli? Tarrantloch wasn't even his to lose! It was supposed to be held in trust for her until she turned twenty-five, less than a year from now.

Her sanctuary. Her private bolthole. The one place she could be herself without hundreds of cameras flashing in her face.

Gone. Lost. Gambled away.

Now it was in the hands of her mortal enemy.

Oh, how Remy would be gloating! She could picture him in her mind: that cocky smirk of victory on his sensual mouth; those dark espresso-brown eyes glinting.

Oh, how her blood boiled!

He would be strutting around the whole of Europe telling everyone how he had finally got the better of Henri Marchand.

The bitter rivalry between her father and the Caffarellis went back a decade. Remy's grandfather Vittorio had been best friends and business partners with her father, but something had soured the relationship and at the last minute Henri had pulled out of a major business development he had been bankrolling for Vittorio. The Caffarellis' financial empire had been severely compromised, and the two men hadn't spoken a word to each other since.

Angelique had long expected it would be Remy who would pursue her father for revenge and not one of his brothers. Of the three Caffarelli brothers, Remy had had the most to do with his grandfather, but their relationship wasn't affectionate or even close. She suspected Remy was after his grandfather's approval, to win his respect, something neither of his older brothers had been able to do in spite of creating their own massive fortunes independent of the family empire.

But Angelique had clashed with Remy even before the fallout between their families and his dealings with her father. She thought him spoilt and reckless. He thought her attention-seeking. The eight-year difference in their ages hadn't helped, although she was the first to admit she hadn't been an easy person to be around, particularly after her mother had died.

Angelique turned back to her father who was washing the bitter taste of defeat down with a generous tumbler of brandy. 'Mum's probably spinning in her grave—and her parents and grandparents along with her. How could you be so…so *stupid*?'

Henri's eyes hardened and his thin lips thinned and whitened. 'Watch your mouth, young lady. I am your father. You will not speak to me as if I am an imbecile.'

She squared her shoulders and steeled her spine. 'What are you going to do? Call me a whole lot of nasty names like you did to Mum? Verbally and emotionally abuse me until I take an overdose just to get away from you?'

The silence was thick, pulsing, almost vibrating with menace.

Angelique knew it was dangerous to upset her father. To mention what must never be mentioned.

She had spent her childhood walking around on tiptoe to avoid triggering his ire. His temper could be vicious. As a young child she had witnessed how her mother's self-esteem had been eroded away, leaving her a wilted shadow of her former self.

But, while her father had never raised a hand either to her mother or to Angelique, the potential threat of it was there all the same. It hovered in the atmosphere. It crawled along her skin like a nasty, prickly-footed insect.

In the early years Angelique had tried hard to please him but nothing she had ever done had been good enough, or at least not good enough for his impossibly exacting standards.

In the end she had decided to do the opposite. Since the age of seventeen she had deliberately set out to embarrass him. To shock him. That was why she had pursued her career as a swimsuit model so determinedly. She knew how much it annoyed and embarrassed him that his little girl's body was displayed in magazines, catalogues and billboards all over Europe. She had even deliberately courted scandals in the press, not caring that they further cemented her reputation as a wild, spoilt little rich girl who loved nothing more than to party, and to party hard.

'If you're not careful I will disinherit you.' Her father issued the threat through clenched teeth. 'I will give every penny away to a dog's home.'

Angelique would have said, "Go on. Do it," but the fortune he threatened to give away had actually belonged to her mother. And she was going to do her darned hardest to get back what was rightfully hers.

Starting now.

The desert of Dharbiri was one of Remy's favourite places. One of his friends from his boarding-school days, Talib Firas Muhtadi, was a crown prince of the ancient province. The golden stretch of endless wind-rippled sands, the lonely sound of the whistling, pizza-oven-hot air; the vibrant colours of the sunset; the sense of isolation and the almost feudal laws and customs were such a stark change from his thoroughly modern twenty-first-century life.

No alcohol. No gambling. No unchaperoned women.

He loved his fast-paced life—there was absolutely no doubt about that—it was just that now and again he felt the need to unplug himself from it and recharge his batteries.

The hot, dry air was such a contrast to the chill of autumn that had come early back in Italy where he had spent a couple of days with his grandfather. No matter the season, Vittorio was a difficult person to be around, bitter and even at times violent. But Remy liked the sense of power it gave him to drop in with-out notice—which he knew annoyed the hell out of his grandfather—stay a couple of days and then breeze off without saying goodbye.

But while Remy loved Italy it was hard to decide where he felt most at home. His French-Italian heritage, on top of his English boarding-school education, had more or less made him a citizen of the world. Up until now he hadn't really had a base to call home. He'd lived in and out of suitcases and hotel suites. He liked that he didn't know where he was going to be from one week to the next. He would pick up a scent like a foxhound and go after a good deal. And nail it.

He liked to move around the globe, picking up busi-ness here and there, wheeling and dealing, winning the unwinnable.

He grinned.

Like winning that winner-takes-all hand with Henri Marchand in Vegas. It had been a masterstroke of genius on his part. He didn't like to be *too* smug about it but, truth be told, he did actually feel a little bit proud of himself.

He'd hit Henri Marchand where it hurt: he had taken that double-crossing cheat's Scottish castle off him.

Victory was more than sweet—it was ambrosial.

Remy had come out to Dharbiri so he could reflect on his prize. Tarrantloch was one of the most beautiful and prestigious estates in Scotland. It was isolated and private. It would make a fabulous base for him—a place he could call home. It would be the perfect haven to hunt, shoot, fish and hang out with his friends during his infamous week-long parties. He could have gone straight there to take ownership but he didn't want to appear *too* eager to take possession.

No, it was better to let Henri Marchand—and his spoilt little brattish daughter Angelique—think this was just like any other deal done and dusted.

There would be plenty of time to rub her retroussé little nose in it.

He couldn't wait.

Getting a flight to Dharbiri was hard enough. Getting access to where Remy Caffarelli was staying was like trying to get through an airport security check-in with a fistful of grenades or an AK47 in her hand luggage.

Angelique ground her teeth for the tenth time. Did she *look* like a security threat?

'I need to speak to Monsieur Caffarelli. It's a matter of great urgency. A family…er, crisis.'

Her family crisis.

The attendant on the reception desk was cool and disbelieving. Angelique could only suppose he was used to fielding off droves of female wannabes who would give an arm or a leg—or both—to have a few minutes with the staggeringly rich, heart-stoppingly gorgeous Remy Caffarelli.

As if *she* would ever sink so low.

'Monsieur Caffarelli is not available right now.' The attendant gave her a look that immediately categorised her as just another hopeful, starry-eyed wannabe. 'He is dining with the Crown Prince and his wife, and according to royal protocol he cannot be interrupted unless it is a matter of utmost political urgency.'

Angelique mentally rolled her eyes. It looked like she would have to try another tactic; find some other way of getting under the radar. But she was good at that sort of thing.

Outsmarting. Outmanoeuvring. Outwitting.

She smiled to herself.

That was her speciality.

It didn't take long to bribe a junior housemaid who recognised Angelique from a magazine shoot she'd done a couple of months ago. All it took was an autograph to get access to Remy's suite.

The young housemaid had mentioned how important it was Angelique wasn't seen in Remy's room other than by Remy himself. Apparently there were strict protocols on women and men socialising without appropriate supervision. As much as it annoyed her to have to hide until she knew for sure it was Remy entering the suite, Angelique decided to play things safe.

She scanned the room for a suitable hiding place.

Behind the curtains? No; she would be seen from outside.

The bathroom? No; a housemaid might come in to clean up the appalling mess Remy had left there.

Angelique looked at the wall-to-ceiling wardrobe running along one wall.

A little clichéd perhaps…

But perfect!

CHAPTER TWO

REMY FELT A strange sense of disquiet as soon as he entered his suite; unease; a sense that the place was not quite the way he had left it. He had cancelled the evening housekeeping visit because he hated people fussing around him all the time. Surely they hadn't gone against his wishes?

He closed the door and stilled.

Waited.

Listened.

His gaze scanned the luxuriously appointed suite for any signs of a disturbance. His laptop was still open on the desk and the screensaver was the same as when he'd left to have dinner. The can of soda he had half-drunk was still sitting where he'd left it, and a ring of moisture from the condensation had pooled around the bottom.

His gaze went further, to the open door of the palatial bedroom. The bed cover was slightly crumpled from where he had sat while he'd taken a call from one of his office staff in Monte Carlo. One of the towels he'd used when he'd showered was still lying on the floor. The clothes he'd worn earlier were in a messy pile nearby.

It was jet lag, that was all. He gave himself a mental shake, shrugged off his dinner jacket and threw it over the arm of the nearest sofa. He reached up and loosened his tie. It had been feeling a little tight all evening, but rules were rules, and he was happy to go along with them because out here he could forget he was the youngest son of the Caffarelli dynasty.

Here there was no one measuring him up against his older brothers or his impossible-to-please grandfather.

Out here he was as free as a desert falcon. He had the next few days to kick back and chill out in one of the hottest places on earth. Life could be pretty good when *he* was in the driving seat.

Angelique held her breath for so long she thought she would faint. But she knew she had to wait until Remy was well and truly inside the suite and in a relaxed mood before she came out of the closet—so to speak.

Not that there were too many of his clothes *in* the closet.

Most of them seemed to be on the floor of the bedroom or spilling haphazardly out of his lightweight travel bag. The en suite bathroom she'd scoped out earlier was just as bad. He'd left a dark ring of stubble in the marble basin when he'd shaved and there had been yet another wet towel on the floor.

It confirmed what she already knew: Remy Caffarelli was a spoilt playboy with more money than sense who had grown up with servants dancing around to satisfy his every whim.

It was a tiny bit ironic of her to point the finger at such a shiny black kettle as Remy when she too had grown up surrounded by wealth. But at least she knew how to pick up after herself and she could cook a three-course gourmet meal with one arm and her appetite tied behind her back.

Remy had never even boiled an egg.

He had probably never even boiled a kettle!

Angelique clenched her fists and her jaw.

He just boiled her blood.

She heard him moving about the suite. She heard the ring pull of a can being opened. It couldn't be alcohol, as this was a totally dry province. There were stiff penalties for bringing in or consuming contraband liquor.

She heard the click of his laptop being activated and then the sound of his fingers typing on the keyboard. She heard him a give a deep, throaty chuckle as if something he'd just read online or in an email had amused him.

Her belly gave a little flip-flop movement.

He had a *very* nice laugh. He had a *very* nice smile. He had a *very* nice mouth. She had spent most of her teenage years fantasising about that mouth.

Stop it right now, you silly little fool!

You are not going to think about his mouth, or any other part of his totally hot, totally amazing body.

Just as Angelique was about to step out of the wardrobe, she heard a sharp, businesslike knock at the door of the suite. Her heart gave a jerky kick against her breastbone.

Was he expecting someone?

One of his star-struck wannabes, perhaps? Oh God! If she had to listen to him having bed-wrecking sex with some bimbo who had been smuggled into his room…

'Monsieur Caffarelli?' an official-sounding voice called out. 'We wish to have a word with you.'

She heard Remy's footsteps as he moved across to open the door. 'Yes?' he said in that charming, 'I'm happy to help you' way he had down to a science.

The official cleared his throat as if he found what he was about to say quite difficult. 'We have received some information that you have a young woman in your room.'

'Pardon?' Remy's predominantly French accent made Angelique's belly do another little tumble.

'As you are well aware, Monsieur Caffarelli, the dictates of our province state that no single woman must be unchaperoned with a man unless she is his sister or his wife. We have reason to believe you have someone in your room who does not fit either of those categories.'

'Are you out of your mind?' Remy sounded incredulous. 'I know the rules. I've been coming here long enough. I would never do anything to insult Sheikh Muhtadi. Surely his officials—including you—know that?'

'A junior member of our housekeeping staff has tearfully confessed to allowing a young woman access to your room,' the official said. 'We wish to check on whether this is true or not.'

'Go on. Check.' Remy sounded supremely, arrogantly confident. 'You won't find anyone in here but me.'

Angelique heard the door of the suite being flung open and her breath screeched to a skidding halt in her throat. Her heart was pounding like a sledgehammer on a rocky surface. It actually felt like it was going to leap out of her chest. She shrank back inside the closet, hoping the shadows of the space would conceal her. She even closed her eyes, just like a little child playing hide and seek, thinking that if she couldn't see them, they couldn't see her.

She heard firm footsteps moving about the suite, doors being opened and closed. The curtains were swished back. Even the drawers of Remy's desk were opened and then shut.

A drawer? They thought she could fit in a *drawer*?

'See?' Remy's tone had a touch of irritability to it now. 'There's no one here but me.'

'The closet.' The more senior of the two officials spoke. Angelique could almost picture him giving a brisk nod towards her hidey-hole. 'Check the bedroom closet.'

'Are you joking?' Remy coughed out a laugh. 'Do you *really* think I would do something as clichéd as that?'

The mirrored door slid back on its tracks. Angelique raised her right hand and gave a little fingertip wave. 'Surprise!'

Remy could not believe his eyes. He blinked to make sure he wasn't imagining things. That could *not* be Angelique Marchand in his closet.

He opened his eyes and looked again.

It was.

'What the hell are you doing?' He glared at her so fiercely his eyes ached. 'What are the hell are you doing in my room? In my closet?'

She stepped out of the closet as if she was stepping out on to one of the catwalks she frequented all over Europe. She moved like a sinuous cat, all legs, arms, high, pert breasts and pouting full-lipped mouth. Her distinctive grey-blue eyes gave him a reproving look. 'That's not a very nice welcome, Remy. I thought you had better manners than that.'

Remy had never thought he had a temper until he'd had to deal with Angelique. He could feel his rage building up inside him like a cauldron on the boil. No one made him angrier than she did. She was willful, spoilt and a little too determined to get her own way. Did she have no sense of protocol or politeness? What the hell was she doing here? And in his room?

Did she have any idea of the trouble she could get him into?

She had made him look like a liar. Trust was everything in a place like Dharbiri. He might be a friend of the Crown Prince but flouting the rules out here was a definite no-no, friend or foe.

He could be deported.

Charged.

The blood suddenly ran ice-cold in his veins.

Flogged.

'You had better have a very good explanation for why you're in my room,' he said through gritted teeth.

She swept her thick, wavy, glossy black mane of hair over one slim shoulder. 'I came to see you about my house. You *have* to give it back.' She nailed him with a look that was diamond-hard. 'I'm not leaving your side until you sign me over the deeds to Tarrantloch.'

'Monsieur Caffarelli,' the older official spoke in a stern 'don't mess with me' tone. 'Would you please verify if this young woman is personally known or related to you? If not we will have her immediately evicted and the authorities will deal with her accordingly.'

Deal with her? Remy didn't like the sound of that. As much as he hated Angelique, he could not stand by and see her come to any harm. He took a deep breath and put on his best 'let's be cool about this' smile. 'I'm afraid there's been a little mix-up. I had no idea my fiancée was going to surprise me by turn—'

'Your fiancée?' Angelique and the senior official spoke in unison.

Remy gave the official a conciliatory smile. 'We've been trying to keep our engagement a secret. The press make such of fuss of this stuff at home.' He gave a Gallic shrug. 'You know how it is.'

The official straightened his shoulders, his expression as formal as a drill sergeant. 'This young woman may well be your fiancée, but it is against the laws of our land for her to be alone with you without a chaperone.'

'So, we'll get a chaperone,' Remy said. 'She won't be with me long in any case, will you, *ma chérie*?'

Angelique's eyes narrowed to hairpin slits but her voice had a false sort of sing-song quality to it that grated on Remy's already overstretched nerves. 'Only for as long as it takes, *mon trésor.*'

The official puffed himself up to his not considerable height. 'Due to the circumstances of your fiancée's… ahem…surprise visit, neither of you will be permitted to leave the province until you are legally married.'

'Married?' Angelique had joined Remy in a choked gasp of horror.

'You're joking?' Angelique gaped at the official with wide shocked eyes. 'You *have* to be joking!'

'He's not joking,' Remy muttered just low enough for her to hear it. 'Go along with it. Try and keep cool.'

Keep cool? Who was he kidding? He didn't feel cool. He'd never had to think so fast on his feet in his life. Pretending she was his fiancée had just popped into his head. And it still might not be enough to get them over the line.

'I'm not marrying you!' She flashed him a livid, blue-lightning look. 'I'd rather die!'

'Yes, well, you just might get that choice,' he said. 'We're not in France, Italy or England right now. Didn't you check out the Smart Traveller website before you came?'

Her throat rose and fell. 'I didn't think. I just…'

'Not thinking is something you do remarkably well.' Remy gave her a dressing-down look. 'You've made a lifetime's work of it.'

Her small hands clenched into tight fists and her eyes gave him another deadly glare. 'I thought you were best friends with the Crown Prince. Can't *he* do something?'

'Afraid not.' Remy had already had this debate with his friend during university. 'The royal family have a lot of power but not enough to overrule laws of the elder tribesmen of the province.'

'But that's ridiculous!'

Remy gave her a cautionary look. 'If you're going to stand there spluttering insults like a Roman candle firecracker, I'm not going to lay down my life for you.'

She opened and closed her mouth, seemingly lost for words. Not that it would last. He knew how quick and sharp her tongue could be. She always tried to get the last word.

He was the only person in her life who wouldn't let her have it.

'Monsieur Caffarelli?' The official stepped forward. 'We must leave now to make the necessary arrangements to conduct the ceremony first thing in the morning. We will arrange alternative accommodation for your fiancée. You will understand that she is not permitted to spend the night in your room.'

'But of course.' Remy gave him another charming smile. *I don't want her here in any case.* 'I understand completely. I sincerely apologise for my fiancée's impulsive behaviour. She is a little wilful and headstrong at times, but once we are married she will soon learn to toe the line. I'll make absolutely sure of it.'

Remy smiled to himself when he saw the two red-hot spots of colour pooling in Angelique's cheeks. She was standing rock-steady but he knew her well enough to know she was beyond livid with him. He could see it in her stormy eyes and in the clenched posture of her jaw. Too bad they had to have a chaperone. He would have quite liked to see what that anger looked like when it was finally unleashed.

Angelique turned to look at the senior official, her expression now meek and demure, those thick, impossibly long eyelashes batting up and down for good measure. 'Please may I have a private word with my, er, fiancé? Perhaps you could chaperone us from the lounge. We'll leave the door open here. Would that be acceptable?'

The official gave a formal nod and indicated with a jerk of his head for his sidekick to follow him out to the lounge area.

Remy got the full, fiery force of Angelique's gaze as she swung around to face him once the officials had gone. 'There's no point glaring at me like that,' he said before she could let fly. 'You're the one who brought this about.'

She visibly shook with rage. It reminded him of the shuddering of a small two-stroke engine on the back of a dingy.

'Fiancée?' She sounded like she was choking on the word. 'Why couldn't you have said I was your sister or…or even your cousin?'

'Because the whole world knows I'm one of three brothers who were orphaned when we were young. And since both of my parents were only children, I don't have any cousins.'

Her eyes fired another round of hatred at him. 'Did you have to make that comment about controlling me as if I'm some sort of waspish virago? You did it deliberately, didn't you? You just can't help yourself. Any chance you get, you like to thrust home the chauvinist dagger.'

Right now that wasn't the only thing Remy wanted to thrust home. He had always tried to ignore the sexual attraction he felt for her. In the past she had always been banned by his family or too involved with someone else. But it was hard to ignore the tingling that was stirring in his loins right now.

And if they had been in any other place he might well have done something about it.

'Got under your skin, did it, *ma petite*?'

'You set my father up, didn't you?' Her expression was tight with barely compressed rage. 'I know how your mind works. You wanted to hit him where it hurt most because of that stupid deal in Ibiza. But I'm not letting you get away with it. I'll fight you tooth and nail until you give me back my house.'

Remy gave her a cool and totally unaffected look because he knew how much it would annoy her. 'Fight me all you like. There's no way I'm giving it back. I won it fair and square. Your father knew what he was getting into—he knew the risks he was taking. But I must say, I think it's pretty pathetic of him to send you out here to try and butter me up.'

Her head jerked back. 'You think *that's* why I'm here? As if I would ever sink so low as that. You're the last man on earth I would ever consider seducing.'

'Likewise, *ma coeur*; you don't float my boat, either.'

A flicker of uncertainty came and went in her gaze and her perfectly aligned, beautiful white teeth sank into her bottom lip.

But just for a nanosecond.

She suddenly pulled herself upright, like an abandoned hand puppet that had just been reconnected with a firm hand. 'And as for marriage… Well, that's just totally ridiculous. It's out of the question. I *won't* do it.'

'It'll just be a formality,' Remy said. 'We don't have to take this seriously. It probably won't even be recognised as legal back home. We'll just do what they require and then we'll leave. Simple.'

'*Simple?*' Her eyes shot their fury at him again. 'Tell me what about this is simple. We'll be married—' she gave a little shudder as if the word was anathema to her '—or at least, we will be on paper. I don't care if it's legal or not. I don't want to be married to you. I can't think of anything worse.'

He gave her a smile. 'We'll get it annulled as soon as we get back to Europe.'

'This is outrageous! This is a…a *disaster*!'

'Of your own making.' He used his 'too cool for school' tone again. He loved the way it triggered something feral in her. She went off like a bomb every time.

She flattened her mouth into a thin white line, her eyes looking murderous. 'This is *not* my fault. This is *your* fault for being so determined to score points. You don't need Tarrantloch; your family have properties bigger and better than that all over the world. Why did you have to take the one thing I love more than anything else?'

Remy felt a little niggle of guilt. Just a niggle; nothing major. Nothing he couldn't ignore.

He'd set himself a goal and he'd achieved it.

That was the Caffarelli credo—goal; focus; win.

Remy could have taken any one of the businesses in the Marchand Holdings portfolio if he'd been so inclined, but Tarrantloch was the one thing he knew Henri

Marchand would regret losing the most. He had a score to settle with Henri that had nothing to do with his grandfather's dealings with him.

It was far more personal.

Remy had just about got the Ibiza development in the bag when an anonymous email had spooked the vendor. It hadn't been too hard to find out who had sent it. Henri Marchand was devious but not particularly smart at covering his tracks. Remy had sworn he would get revenge, no matter how long it took.

Tarrantloch was Henri Marchand's most valued, prized possession. It was his ultimate status symbol. Henri liked to play Laird of the Highlands with a coterie of his overfed, overindulged, overweight corporate cronies by his side.

The fact that his daughter—his only child and heir— fancied herself in love with the place didn't come into it at all.

Not even a niggly bit.

Remy was running a business, not a charity, and the one person in the world he felt the least charitable towards was Angelique Marchand.

'It's mine now. Get over it.' He refused to allow sentimentality to mess with his head. 'It's not like you'll be homeless. You live in Paris most of the year, don't you?'

Her expression was so rigid with anger he could see a muscle moving in and out in her cheek. 'I planned to live at Tarrantloch after my retirement.'

He whistled through his teeth. 'That's some seriously long-term planning. You're what, twenty-five?'

Her teeth made a grinding noise. 'Twenty-four. I'll be twenty-five next year in May.'

'So, what age do swimsuit models retire?' He couldn't

stop his gaze sweeping over her body. To say she had a knockout figure was a bit of an understatement.

More than a bit, actually.

He could not think of a body he found more delightful to look at. Distracting. He had been distracted by it for the last few years, and so too had just about everyone throughout Europe. He still remembered the first time he had driven past a billboard with the then-nineteen-year-old Angelique on it. She had been draped along the edge of an infinity pool in some exotic tropical location, wearing a couple of miniscule triangles of fabric that left just enough to the imagination to cause serious discomfort in his nether regions.

To say she had a traffic-stopping figure was putting it rather mildly.

'I want to branch out into other areas of the business,' she said.

'Such as?'

She glowered at him. 'I'm not going to discuss my career plans with you. You'll just rubbish them. You'll tell me I'm wasting my time or to go and get a real job or something.'

Remy felt that little niggle of guilt again. He hadn't been exactly encouraging of her plans to pursue a modelling career. When he'd first heard she was going to quit school to sign up with a modelling agency, he'd put aside his grandfather's ban on contact with her and had called and told her to reconsider.

But listening to advice was not something Angelique was particularly good at doing.

'Monsieur Caffarelli?' The official spoke from the open doorway. 'The room is now ready for your fiancée.' He turned to Angelique. 'If you will come this way, *mademoiselle*? We have two chaperones to accompany you.'

Angelique glared at Remy as she stalked past him. He caught a whiff of her signature fragrance as she went by. It hovered about his nostrils, enticing him to breathe in deep. He had always associated the smell of sweetpeas with her—strong, heady and colourful.

His brain snapped back to attention like an elastic band being flicked by a finger.

Within hours they would be man and wife.

Usually whenever the 'M' word was mentioned to him he had a standard, stock phrase: *over my dead body*.

But somehow—right here and now—it didn't have quite the same ring to it.

CHAPTER THREE

ANGELIQUE COULD NOT even close her eyes, let alone get to sleep. She spent most of the night pacing the floor, cursing Remy, *hating* him. How could he have done this to her? He couldn't have thought of a worse punishment.

Married.

To him of all people!

It didn't matter if it was legal or not. She had sworn she would *never* marry. She would never allow someone else to have that sort of control over her, to have that sort of *commitment* from her.

She had seen first-hand her mother's commitment. Kate Tarrant had taken her marriage vows way too seriously. She had been browbeaten and submissive from day one. She had toed the line. She had obeyed. She had given up her freedom and her sense of self.

Angelique would *never* do that.

Marriage and all it represented nauseated her. Unlike most girls her age, she couldn't even bear the thought of wedding finery. Who wanted to dress up like a meringue, be smothered in a veil and be given away like a parcel to some man who would spend the next fifty years treating her like a household slave?

There was a knock on the door and when she opened it she found a maid holding a tray with fresh fruit, rolls and steaming hot, rather unusually fragrant coffee. 'Your breakfast, *mademoiselle*.'

Was this the time to announce that—despite her half-French bloodline—she actually loathed coffee and could only ever face tea first thing in the morning?

Probably not.

Not long after that maid left, another one much older one arrived, carrying a massive armful of wedding finery which she informed Angelique she would help her get into in preparation for the ceremony at ten.

'I'm not wearing that!' Angelique said as the maid laid out an outfit that looked more like a circus tent. A particularly beautiful circus tent, however. On closer inspection she saw there were fine threads of gold delicately woven into the fabric and hundreds of diamonds were stitched across the bodice.

'These are the official bridal robes of the province,' the maid said. 'The Princess Royal was married in them in July. It is a great honour that you have been given permission to wear them.'

I can't believe I'm doing this, Angelique thought as she stood and was wrapped in the voluminous folds. The irony wasn't lost on her. She made a living out of wearing the minimum of fabric. Now she was being wrapped in metres of it like some sort of glittering present.

Her blood simmered.

It boiled.

How could it be possible that within a less than an hour she would be married to Remy Caffarelli?

'Are we done?'

'Just about.' The maid came at her with a denser than normal veil dripping with even more diamonds and a train that was at least five metres long.

'Oh no.' Angelique shied away. 'Not that.'

The maid gave her a pragmatic look. 'Do you want to get out of here or don't you?'

'Are you OK with this?' Crown Prince Talib Firas Muhtadi said to Remy as he finished his second cup of thick, rich, aromatic cardamom-scented coffee. 'Things are really unstable right now in our province. The tribal elders are notoriously difficult to negotiate with and highly unpredictable. It's best to do things their way just to be on the safe side. We don't want a major uprising over an incident like this. Best to nip it in the bud and keep everyone happy.'

Remy mentally rolled his eyes as he put his cup back down on the saucer. 'No big deal. It's just a formality, right? It's not like this marriage—' he made the quotation marks with his fingers '—will be recognised at home.'

Talib looked at him for a long moment without speaking.

'You're joking, right?' Remy said, feeling a chill roll down his spine like an ice cube. *Please be joking.*

'Marriage is a very sacred institution in our culture,' Talib said. 'We don't enter into it lightly, nor do we leave it unless there are very good reasons for it.'

What about total unsuitability?

Being polar opposites?

Hating each other?

'I fought it too, Remy,' Talib added. 'But it's only since I met and married Abby that I realised what I've been missing out on. Oh, and yes, the marriage will be considered legal in your country.'

Damn.

Double damn.

* * *

The first thought Remy had was it could be anyone under that traditional wedding dress and long veil and he would not be any the wiser. But he instantly knew it was Angelique because of the way the robes were shaking, as if her rage was barely contained within the diamond-encrusted tent of the fabric that surrounded her slim body.

And her eyes.

How could he not recognise those stormy grey-blue eyes? They flashed with undiluted loathing through the gauze of the veil as she came to stand beside him.

He suddenly had a vision of his oldest brother Rafe's wedding day only a few weeks ago. The ceremony had been very traditional, and his bride, Poppy Silverton, had been quite stunningly beautiful and unmistakably in love. So too had Rafe, which had come as a bit of a surprise to Remy. He'd always thought Rafe was the show-no-emotion, feel-no-emotion type, but he'd actually seen moisture in Rafe's eyes as he'd slipped the wedding band on Poppy's finger, and his face had been a picture of devotion and pride.

His other brother Raoul was heading down the altar too, apparently just before Christmas. His bride-to-be, Lily Archer, had been employed to help rehabilitate Raoul after a water-skiing accident which had left him in a wheelchair. Remy had never seen Raoul happier since he'd announced his engagement to Lily, which was another big surprise, given how physically active Raoul had always been. But apparently love made up for all of that.

Not that Remy would know or ever wanted to know about love. He'd had his fair share of crushes, but as to falling in love…

Well, that was something he stayed well clear of and he intended to keep doing so.

Loving someone meant you could lose them. They could be there one minute and gone the next.

Like his parents.

Remy sometimes found it hard even to remember what his mother and father had looked like unless he jogged his memory with a photo or a home video. He had been seven years old when they had died, and as each year passed his memories of them faded even further. Listening to their voices and seeing them moving about on those home videos still seemed a little weird, as if a tiny part of his brain recognised them as people he had once known intimately but who were now little more than strangers.

He had completely forgotten their touch.

But there was one touch he was not going to forget in a hurry.

As soon as the cleric asked Remy to join hands with Angelique, he felt a lightning zap shoot up his from his hand, travel from the length of his arm and straight to his groin as if she had touched him there with her bare hands. He hadn't touched her even when her father had brought her with him when he had socialised with Remy's grandfather in the years before their fall out. Being eight years older than her, Remy had occasionally been left with the task of entertaining her during one of his grandfather's soirées. Even as a young teenager she had shown the promise of great beauty. That raven-black hair, those bewitching eyes, those lissom limbs and budding breasts had been a potent but forbidden temptation.

He had always made a point of *not* touching her.

Would the cleric expect him to kiss her? Not that

the idea didn't hold a certain appeal, but Remy would rather kiss her in private than in front of a small group of conservative tribesmen.

After all, he didn't want to offend them.

Angelique's hand was tiny. His hand almost swallowed it whole. But then the whole of her was tiny. Dainty. He felt a primal stirring in his loins when he thought of what it might be like to enter her. To possess her. To feel her sexy little body grip him tightly…

Whoa, keep it in your trousers. Remember, this is just an on-paper marriage.

The cleric went through the vows and Remy recited his lines as if he were an actor reading them from a script. No big deal. They were just words. Meaningless words.

When Angelique came to her lines she coughed them out like a cat with fur balls. She almost choked on the promise to obey him.

'I now pronounce you man and wife.' The cleric gave Remy a man-to-man smile. 'You may lift the veil and kiss your bride.'

Angelique's eyes flickered with something that looked like panic. 'I'd really rather not.'

Remy didn't give her time to finish her sentence in case she blew their cover. Besides, he'd kissed dozens of women. All he had to do was plant a perfunctory kiss on her lips and step back. Everyone would be happy.

Easy.

He lifted the heavy veil from her face and planted his mouth on hers.

Angelique had spent years during her teens imagining this very moment—the first time Remy kissed her. She had imagined it when other dates were kissing her, closing her eyes and dreaming it was actually Remy's mouth moving on hers, his hands touching her, his body wanting her. Quite frankly, those mind-wanderings of hers had made some of those kisses—not to mention some of her sexual encounters—a little more bearable.

But not one of her imaginings came anywhere near to the real deal.

Remy didn't kiss sloppily or wetly or inexpertly.

He kissed with purpose and potency.

The firm warmth of his lips, the taste of him, the feel of him was so…so *intensely* male, so addictive, she couldn't stop herself from pushing up on tiptoe to keep the connection going. His mouth hardened and then she felt his tongue push against her lips just as she opened them.

His tongue slid into her mouth and found hers.

She heard him smother a groan as her tongue tangled with his.

She felt his body stir against her as he gripped her by the hips and pulled her flush against him.

She heard the cleric clear his throat. 'Ahem…'

Remy dropped his hands. He looked slightly stunned for a moment, but then he seemed to give himself a mental shake before he grinned charmingly and rather cheekily at the cleric. 'Almost forgot where I was for a moment.'

The cleric gave him an understanding smile. 'It is very good to see an enthusiastic couple. It bodes well for a happy and fulfilling marriage.'

Angelique ground her teeth. Remy was enjoying this much more than he should. She could see the glint in his eyes as they reconnected with hers. She gave him an 'I'll get you for this later' look but he just grinned even wider and gave her a wink.

'The Crown Prince and his wife have a put on a special banquet in honour of your marriage,' the cleric said.

Oh no! Don't tell me there's going to be a reception with speeches.

But as it turned out it was more like a party. A dry party. Which was a crying shame, as right now Angelique needed a glass of something alcoholic—make that two glasses and to hell with the calories—because she was now officially *a married woman.*

Arrrggh!

The reception room was as big as a football field, or so it appeared to Angelique. How many friends did Remy have out here, or had someone rented a crowd? There were at least a thousand people. Who had a wedding that big? It was ridiculous! It was like a wedding extravaganza, a showpiece of what a celebrity wedding reception should be. The room was decked out in the most amazing array of satin ribbons, balloons and sparkly lights that hung from the high ceiling like diamonds. They probably *were* diamonds, she thought as she glanced up at the chandelier above her head. *Yep, diamonds.*

They were led to the top table where Angelique was finally introduced to the Crown Prince's wife, Abby, a fellow Englishwoman who had met and fallen in love with Talib earlier that year. A royal baby was due in a few months, which Abby explained had given an extra boost to the celebrations. It seemed Dharbiri was in party mode and an event like this could on for days. *Great.*

Remy took her hand and led her out to the dance floor for the bridal waltz. 'Loosen up, Angelique. You feel like a shop-window mannequin in my arms.'

Angelique suppressed a glare. 'Get your hands off my butt.'

He smoothed his hand over her hip and then tugged her against him. 'That better?'

She looked at him with slitted eyes. 'We're supposed to be dancing, not making out.'

'I thought you'd be great at dancing.'

'I *am* great at dancing.'

'Then show me your footwork.'

Angelique moved in against him and let him take the lead. The music was romantic with a flowing rhythm so she let her body move in time with it. She started to feel like a princess at a ball, or a star contestant on one of those reality dance shows. They moved in perfect unison around the dance floor. The other couples—and there were hundreds—swarmed backwards to give them more room.

'Nice work,' Remy said once it was over. 'Maybe we should do that again some time.'

'You trod on my toe.'

'Did not.'

'Did so.'

He gave her a grin as he pinched her cheek. 'Smile, *ma chérie.*'

She smiled through clenched teeth. 'I want to scratch your eyes out.'

'Did I tell you how beautiful you looked?'

'I can't breathe in this dress. And I have no idea how I'm going to fit in the bathroom. They'll have to take the door off or something.'

He grinned again and tapped her gently on the end of the nose. 'You'll find a way.'

Angelique let out a breath as she watched him turn

to speak to another guest. There were times when Remy took his charm into very dangerous territory...

'You have to try this,' Remy said as he came over with a loaded plate from the banquet a little while later.

Angelique breathed in the delicious smell of lamb with herbs and garlic. She couldn't stop her gaze from devouring everything on his plate. Along with the juicy lamb pieces, there was a couscous salad and some sort of potato dish and flatbread. The carbs would be astronomical. 'No.' She gave him a tight smile for the sake of anyone watching. 'I'm not hungry.'

'Here.' He forked a piece of lamb and held it in front of her mouth. 'You have to try this. It's amazing.'

'I don't want it.'

His eyes locked on hers, hard, determined. Implacable. 'Open your mouth.'

Angelique's belly shifted at his commanding tone but she was not going to let him win this. This was *her* battle, not his. She was the one who had to keep her body in top shape for her career. She had been counting calories and carbs since she had landed her first contract. Since before that, actually. It was the only thing she could control. She knew what she had to do to keep her body perfect. She was not going to allow anyone, and in particular Remy Caffarelli, to sabotage her efforts.

She gave him a flinty look. 'I said I'm not hungry.'

'You're lying.'

She felt the penetrating probe of his dark-brown eyes as they tussled with hers. Heat came up from deep inside her, a liquid molten heat that had nothing to do with food but everything to with hunger.

Sexual hunger.

Angelique knew one taste would not be enough. She

would end up bingeing on him and then where would that get her?

His kiss had already done enough damage.

And that dirty dance routine...

She could not afford to let herself be that vulnerable again. She was in control of her passions. She did not slavishly follow her desires. She had self-control and discipline.

She did *not* want him or his food or his fancy footwork.

Angelique pulled out an old excuse but a good one; she was nothing if not a great actress when the need arose. She put a hand to her temple and gave him a part-sheepish, part-apologetic look. 'I'm sorry, Remy, it's just I've been fighting a tension headache ever since I got up. Well, actually, I didn't get up, because I didn't go to bed in the first place. I couldn't sleep a wink.'

He studied her for a moment as if weighing up whether to believe her or not. 'Maybe you're dehydrated. Have you had enough to drink?'

'I could kill for a glass of wine.'

He gave her a wry look. 'You could get killed for having it.'

Angelique felt a cold hand of panic clutch at her insides. 'We *are* safe now, aren't we? I mean now we're—' she gave a mental gulp '—married?'

Remy's expression sobered for a moment, which made that fist of panic grip a little tighter. 'We're safe as long as we act as if this is a real marriage. It would be foolish to let our guard down until we're on the plane home.'

Angelique swallowed as she cast a nervous eye over the crowd of people who had joined in the wedding celebration. They looked friendly and innocuous enough, but how could she be sure one or more of them weren't waiting for her to make a slip up?

Her stomach pitched with dread.

Never in her wildest dreams had she ever thought something like this would happen. She had wanted a face-to-face with Remy. She hadn't given a thought to where he was or whom he was with or whether it would be convenient or politic *or safe*. She had focused solely on her goal to get him to hand back the deeds to Tarrantloch.

Now she was pretending to be married to him.

Not pretending, a little voice reminded her. *You* are *married to him.*

Angelique turned back to look up at Remy. 'Why do you come out here? It's not the sort of place I thought you would be drawn to. It doesn't really suit your party-boy image.'

He gave a shrug of one broad shoulder. 'The Crown Prince is a friend of mine. We went to university together. I like to visit him now and again.'

'Do you come here often?' Angelique gave herself a mental kick for not rephrasing that a little less suggestively.

He gave her a wicked look. 'No single, unchaperoned women in my room, remember?'

She compressed her lips. 'I'm being serious. How many times do you, er, visit?'

He put his plate down on a nearby table. 'Not as often as I'd like. I only get out here once a year. Two, if I'm lucky, like this year when I came out for Talib and Abby's wedding.'

Angelique's eyes widened to the size of the plate he'd just put down. 'But...but *why*? What's so great about it?

I don't see anything that's relaxing or beautiful about it. It's just a bunch of boring old sand dunes.'

He put his hand on her elbow and led her away to a quieter area. 'Will you please keep your opinions to yourself until we're out of danger?' he hissed out of the corner of his mouth.

Angelique wriggled out of his hold, not because she found it unpleasant, but because she found she rather liked it. *A lot*. She hadn't realised until now how much she had come to rely on him protecting her. To come to her rescue. She had blundered into a minefield and yet he had remained calm and steady throughout. Even cracking jokes about it.

Was *he* scared?

If so, he had shown little sign of it until now.

'I'm sorry, but I'm not used to this,' she said. 'You've been coming here for ages. This is my first time. I'm what you would call a desert virgin.'

'What about that bikini shot of you I saw in New York a couple of years back? You were draped over a sand dune with a couple of camels in the background.'

Angelique mentally raised her brows. So he'd seen that, had he? And taken note of it. 'It was staged. The sand dunes were in Mexico and the camels were cranky and smelly. One of them even tried to bite me. It was a horrible shoot. The designer was impossible to please and I ended up with a massive migraine from sunstroke.'

A frown appeared between his eyes. 'Why do you do it?'

She felt her back come up. She'd heard this lecture before, too many times to count. The most memorable one had been from him. 'Why do I do what?'

'Model. Put yourself out there in nothing but a couple of scraps of fabric.' His tone sounded starchy and disapproving. Old-fashioned. *Conservative*. 'You're capable of so much more than being some gorgeous too-perfect-to-believe image young guys jerk off to when they're in the shower.'

Angelique gave him an arch look. 'Is that what *you* do?'

His eyes hardened. His mouth flattened. A muscle ticked in his jaw. On-off. On-off. 'No.' His tone was clipped. *Too* clipped. 'I don't think of you like that.'

He was lying.

Just like she had been lying about her hunger.

How…*interesting*.

The thought of him being turned on by *her*, orgasming because of *her*, was deliciously shocking. It made her flesh tingle. It made her juices run. It made her need pulse and ache to feel him come to completion with her, *the real her*, not some airbrushed image that didn't even come close.

Are you out of your mind? The sensible part of her brain kicked in again.

You are not *going to sleep with Remy. Whether he wants to or you want to.*

Angelique looked up at him, noting the dull flush that had flagged both of his aristocratic cheekbones. 'So, when do we get to step out of this charade? We can leave for the airport once this is over, can't we? I've got my bag packed all ready to go. All you have to do is say the word and I'm out of here with bells on. Not the wedding variety, of course.'

His dark-brown eyes seemed to go a shade darker as they held hers. 'We're not leaving tonight.'

Angelique felt that fist of panic come back, but now it was two fists.

Two very big, very *strong* fists.

'But why not? You have a private jet, don't you? You can leave whenever you want.' She swallowed and looked up at him hopefully. Desperately. 'C-can't you?'

Remy turned his back so anyone nearby couldn't see his expression, his voice sounding low and deep, like a rumble of an imminent earthquake under the ocean floor. 'There is a tradition we have to uphold. We can't leave until we officially consummate the marriage.'

Angelique jerked back from him. 'You're joking. You *have* to be joking! There's no way we have to do *that*! How would anyone know if we, um, did it or not?'

He gave her a levelling look. 'We'd have to prove it.'

Her brows went up. Her eyes went wide. Her heart started to gallop. Her inner core got hot. *Very hot.* 'You mean like witnesses or something? Oh my God, I can't believe this! I'm so not a threesome person. I'm not even a twosome person. I—' She clamped her mouth shut. She had given away too much as it was.

'We'll need evidence that you're a virgin.'

Angelique blinked. *'Pardon?'*

'Blood.' He had his poker face on. 'On the sheets. We have to display them the next morning.'

She gave him a narrowed look. 'Whose blood?'

His mouth cracked in a half-smile. 'Yours.'

Angelique sent him a fulminating glare. 'I just *knew* you were going to say that. The only blood I want to see spilled right now is yours.'

'You're really hating this, aren't you?' His expression was amused.

Her eyes went to slits again. 'By "this" I suppose you mean this ridiculous subservience.'

He gave one of his loose, get-over-it shrugs. 'It's the way things are done here.'

She shook with outrage. 'But it's the wrong way!'

'The women here are happy.' His voice was calm, measured. 'They don't have to do anything but be who they are. They don't have to primp and preen. They don't have to have a spray tan every week or put on false nails or colour their hair. They don't have to pretend they're not hungry when they're starving, because they're not going to be judged solely on their appearance. It is who they are on the inside that matters.'

He was describing a paradise...or was he?

She set her mouth. 'That's only because they probably don't know what they're missing. If just one woman gets a glimpse of what she could have, you could have total anarchy out here.'

An amused quirk tilted his mouth. 'And I suppose you'd be out front and leading the charge of that particular riot?'

She gave him a beady look. 'You'd better believe it.'

CHAPTER FOUR

REMY WAS ENJOYING every minute of his 'marriage' so far. It was so amusing to press all of Angelique's hot buttons. He knew exactly what to say and how to say it—even the way to look at her to get a rise out of her. The reason he knew was because deep down he felt exactly the same.

Marriage was a trap.

It was stultifying. Restraining. A freedom-taking institution that worked better for some than for others.

And he was one of the others.

He didn't like answering to anyone. He had spent too much of his life living under the shadow of his brothers and his grandfather. He wanted to make his own way, to be his own person. To be known as something more than a Caffarelli brother or grandson.

He didn't want to be someone's husband.

And as for being someone's father... Well, he was leaving that to his two older brothers, who seemed pretty keen on the idea of procreating.

Remy was not interested in babies with scrunched-up faces and dirty nappies; sleepless nights, running noses, temper tantrums. Not for him. *No way.*

He was interested in having a good time. Playing

the field. Working the turf. Sowing his oats—the wild variety, that was.

And at times his life could get pretty wild.

He loved the element of risk in what he did—scoping out failing businesses, taking chances, rolling the dice. Chasing success, running it down, holding it in his hands and relishing the victory of yet another deal signed and delivered.

He was a gambler at heart, but not an irresponsible one. He knew where to draw the line, how to measure the stakes and to raise or lower them when he needed to.

And he was a firm believer in the golden rule of gambling: he only ever lost what he could afford to lose.

Besides, he'd already suffered the worst loss of all. Losing his parents so suddenly had been shattering. He still remembered the crushing sense of loss when Rafe had told him about their parents' accident: the panic; the fear; the terror. It had made Remy feel that life was little more than a roll of a dice. Fate was a cruel mistress. Your life could be perfect and full one day, and terrifyingly empty the next.

Remy looked down at Angelique who was trying to disguise her fury at the little 'proof of virginity' story he'd spun her. He wondered how long he could spin it out. She looked so infuriated he thought she was going to explode. She probably had no idea how gorgeous she looked when she was spitting at him like a wild cat. He wouldn't mind having those sharp little claws digging into his back as he rocked them both to paradise.

Are you out of your mind?

If you sleep with her you won't be able to annul the marriage as soon as you get home.

Right. They would have to share a room—there

would be no avoiding that—but he could always sleep on the sofa.

There had better be a sofa or you're toast.

'Right.'

Angelique looked up at him and Remy realised he'd spoken aloud. 'Pardon?' she said.

'How's your headache?'

She looked at him blankly for a moment. 'My...? Oh yes; terrible. Absolutely excruciating.' She put a hand to her temple again. 'I'm getting blurred vision and I think I'm seeing an aura.'

'We'd better get you to bed, then.'

The words dropped into the silence, suspended there, echoing with erotic undercurrents that were impossible to ignore.

'To sleep,' Remy said. 'Just in case you were getting the wrong idea.' Like his body had. It was already hard. Getting harder. *Deep breath.*

She angled her head at him suspiciously. 'Why do I get the feeling you're playing with me?'

He wanted to play with her all right. His body said yes but his mind kept saying no, or at least it was saying no so far. But how long would he be able to keep his hands off her? Theoretically she was the last woman in the world he wanted anything to do with. She was too high-maintenance. Too wild.

But, theory aside, when it came down to practice, well, he was only human. And she *was* hot. He normally preferred blondes but there was something about Angelique's raven hair and creamy skin that had a touch of old-world Hollywood glamour about it. She walked into a room like a movie star. He didn't think it was put on or something she'd learned on the catwalk. He'd seen her do it since she was a kid. *She made an entrance.* It was like she was making a statement: *I'm here. What are you going to do about it?*

She was here all right.

She was right, smack bang in the middle of his life and he couldn't wait to get her out of it.

'You take life too seriously, Angelique.'

'That stuff about the sheets...' She chewed her bottom lip for a moment. 'That's not really true, is it?'

Remy felt a sudden urge to ruffle her hair or pinch her cheeks like he would a little kid. She was so cute when she let her guard down. He couldn't remember ever seeing her look that vulnerable and uncertain before. Angry, annoyed, irritated, yes—but vulnerable? No. If she felt it, she covered it well, but then who was he to talk?

'Why?' He kept his face deadpan. 'Aren't you still a virgin?'

She gave him a pert look. 'Aren't you?'

He laughed. 'An emotional one, maybe, in that I've never been in love. But I've been around a few times.'

She gave her eyes a little roll. 'I can just imagine.'

'How many?'

'How many...what?'

'Lovers.'

She stilled, every muscle on her face seeming to momentarily freeze. But then she gave a little toss of her head and sent him haughty look. 'I fail to see why that should be of any interest to you.'

'I'm your husband.'

One.

Two.

Three.

Blast off.

Remy could time her down to a nanosecond. Her face

went rigid again, her teeth clenching together, her eyes flashing at him like a turbulent gun-metal-grey ocean. 'You're enjoying every minute of this, aren't you?' she hissed at him. 'I bet you can't wait to get back to Italy or France, or wherever it is you live these days, to tell everyone how you tricked me into marrying you. You'll be dining out on this and how you got Tarrantloch off my father for decades, won't you?'

'Calm down.' Remy held up a hand like a stop sign. 'I'm not the one who brought about this marriage. You're the last person I would consider marrying if I was considering marriage, which I'm not, nor ever will be.'

'Ditto.'

'Fine. Then at least we're square on that.' He pushed his sleeve back and glanced impatiently at his watch. 'I think it's time this party was over. Come on. Let's get out of here.'

Angelique followed him with feigned meekness as they said their goodnights to the other guests and officials. Her little white lie about her headache was now lamentably and rather painfully true. Her temples were pounding by the time she got to the suite with Remy. She felt nauseous and lightheaded and her heart began to pound once he closed the door and they were finally alone.

Alone.

In the bridal suite.

She affected a light and breezy tone. 'Do you want to toss a coin for the bed?'

His dark-brown eyes looked darker than they had during the reception. She couldn't make out the shape of his irises at all. He took a coin out of his pocket without breaking his gaze from hers and laid it on the back of his left hand, covered by his right. 'Heads or tails?'

'Heads.'

He flipped the coin high in the air and deftly caught it as it came back down, his gaze still locked on hers. 'Want to change your mind?'

Angelique raised her chin. 'Once my mind is made up I *never* change it.'

His mouth kicked up a little on one side, those dark-chocolate eyes gleaming. 'Ditto.'

She leaned forward to see how the coin had fallen but he hadn't uncovered it. He held it in his closed palm in the space between them. 'Go on. Show me.' Her voice sounded huskier than normal but she put that down to the fact he was in her personal body space. She could smell his citrus, wood and male smell. She could see the rise of fresh dark stubble on his jaw.

She could feel his desire.

It was pulsing in the air like sound waves. There was an answering throb in her body like an echo. Her inner core shifted. Tensed. Clenched. *Hungered.*

She suddenly became aware of her breasts inside the lacy cage of her bra. She became aware of her tongue as it moved out over her lips, depositing moisture to their surface. She saw his hooded gaze follow its passage and something in her stomach unfurled, as if a satin ribbon was being pulled out of its centre.

She took a little swallow. 'Um…the coin?'

His gaze was still fixated on her mouth as if it were the most fascinating mouth in the whole wide world. 'What about it?' His voice sounded deep and rough around the edges.

'I want to know who won.'

'I did.'

Angelique frowned at his confident tone. 'You can't possibly know that without looking.'

His mouth went up at the corners again. 'I have a sixth sense about this sort of stuff. I won. You lost.'

She coughed out a little sound of scorn. 'You think I'm going to fall for that without seeing the evidence? Open your palm.'

His eyes locked back on hers; they seemed to be glinting at the challenge she had laid down. 'Want to make me?' he said.

The floor of her belly shivered. He was near to impossible to resist in this mood. Was that how he bedded so many women? No wonder they fell like ninepins around him. He was just simply irresistible in this playful mood.

But Angelique didn't do alpha males and Remy was very definitely an alpha male. It was in his blood. Had been born and bred to rule, to take charge, to take control and hold onto it no matter what. To lead, not to follow. He was too commanding, too sure of himself, too ruthless and way too sexy.

Too much a Caffarelli.

Too much of an enemy.

Too much of everything.

She hitched up her chin and squared her shoulders. 'Thanks but no.'

His eyes glinted some more, moving slowly between her mouth and her gaze, burning, searing all the way. 'Shame. I was looking forward to a little tussle for possession. It could've been fun.'

Angelique knew he wasn't talking about the coin. She blew out an uneven breath. 'You have the bed. You're much taller than me.' That was an understatement. He'd had to stoop through every door they'd been through so far. 'I can curl up on the sofa.'

'What sofa?'

She chewed her lip as she glanced around the suite. It had everything *but* a sofa. 'Oh… Well, then…'

'The bed is big enough for both of us. You stick to your side. I'll stick to mine. It's only for one night.'

Angelique tried to read his expression but he had his poker face back on. 'I hope you don't snore or talk in your sleep.'

'If I do just give me a shove in the ribs.'

She gave him a frosty look. 'I'm not going to go anywhere near you.'

A sexy smile tilted his mouth. 'Then you'd be the first woman I've shared a bed with who hasn't.'

Angelique spent an inordinate amount of time in the *en suite* cleansing her face and brushing her teeth. She even brushed her hair for a hundred strokes to delay going back into the bedroom. But when she came out of the bathroom there was no sign of Remy. He hadn't even bothered to leave her a note to tell her where he had gone or when he would be back… Or whom he was with.

Careful; you're starting to sound like a wife.

She shook off the thought and pulled back the covers on the massive bed. The tension of the last twenty-four hours—seventy-two if she counted the time since she'd found out Tarrantloch had been lost—had finally caught up with her. As soon as her limbs felt the smooth, cool embrace of the impossibly fine linen she felt every muscle in her body let go. She melted into the mattress, even though it was far too firm for her, and closed her eyes on an exhausted sigh…

* * *

Remy came back to the suite at three in the morning to find Angelique fast asleep.

Right in the middle of the bed.

Her mane of glossy black hair surrounded her head like a cloud. Her blood-red lips were soft and slightly parted, her skin now without its armour of artfully applied make-up. Now she had lost the layer of worldly sophistication she looked young and tiny, almost fragile. There were dark shadows underneath her eyes that her make-up must have hidden earlier. Her slim body—personally he thought she was *too* slim—was curled up like a comma, the sharpness of her hipbone jutting out from beneath the covering of the bed linen.

He could see the spaghetti-thin straps of her nightie, an ivory white that was a perfect foil for the creamy tone of her skin. The upper curves of her breasts were showing just above the sheet. He'd always thought of them as Goldilocks breasts—not too big, not too small, but just right.

He gave himself a mental shake and turned away from the sight of the temptation lying there.

Hands off, remember?

He rubbed a tired hand over the back of his head and down to the knotted muscles in his neck. He'd had to pull some strings to get out of Dharbiri by first light. He didn't want to spend any more time than he had to 'married' to her. If the press got wind of this back home, it would go viral in no time. He didn't want to be made into a laughing stock. He could just imagine the headlines: *World's biggest playboy gets hitched. The last of the Caffarelli rakes bites the dust.*

He wanted to erase it from the record. Wipe it from his memory. Get back to normal.

Get her out of his life.

Remy looked at her again. She murmured something in her sleep and stretched out her arms and legs like a cat—and not just any old moggy—a beautiful, exotic cat that was begging to be stroked.

He wondered who her latest lover was. He hadn't read anything just lately in the press about her, which was surprising, as hardly a month or two went by without some mention of her caught up in some scandal or other. He often wondered how much of it was true. He knew from his own experience that not everything that was reported was accurate. But how she was keeping her head below the parapet was a mystery if not a miracle. It was not an easy feat to stay under the radar when around every corner was a camera phone. You didn't have to be a member of the paparazzi to get a shot of a celebrity or any other high profile person these days.

He'd had a few candid camera shots he'd rather weren't out in the public domain. The press always made it look far worse than it was. He wasn't a heavy drinker, and he had never and would never touch party drugs. But somehow he had been portrayed as a hard-partying, hard-drinking playboy.

The playboy bit was true.

He wasn't going to deny the fact he'd bedded a lot of women. And he wasn't going to stop any time soon. Which was why he had to get this marriage annulled as soon as possible. Call him old-fashioned but, on-paper marriage or no, he was not going to betray those promises he'd made. As far as he was concerned, infidelity was a deal breaker even in his most casual relationships. Sleeping around on a partner was not what a real man would do.

Talking of sleeping… He smothered a yawn as he

heeled off his shoes and unbuttoned his shirt. He tossed it in the vague direction of a chair and put his hands on the waistband of his trousers.

Nah, better keep them on.

He could do with a few more barriers between him and Sleeping Beauty right now. He just hoped two layers—three, if you counted hers—would be enough to keep him out of danger.

CHAPTER FIVE

ANGELIQUE ROLLED OVER and breathed in the scent of lavender-scented sheets, citrus and wood and…warm, sleepy male.

Her heart gave a little flip-flop as she looked at the tanned arm lying across her stomach. It looked so dark, hairy and foreign against the ivory white of her satin nightie. It felt like an iron bar was holding her in place.

His strongly muscled legs were entangled with hers, just loosely, but they felt rough and strong. Powerful.

Had they…? She gulped. *Had sex?*

No.

No!

Hang on a minute… Her body didn't feel any different. She knew without a doubt she would feel *very* different if Remy had made love to her.

She would feel…*satisfied.*

Because she couldn't imagine him not doing the job properly. There would be no half-measures with him. He would know his way around a woman's body like a curator knew their way around a museum. Interesting—some might say Freudian—choice of metaphor, as it felt like an aeon since she'd been intimate with anyone; but still.

Sex had always been a bit of a disappointment to her.

She tried to enjoy it but she had never felt truly comfortable with any of her partners. Not that she'd had as many as the press liked to make out.

Her first experience of sex had been when she had gone to New York to sign with the agency. A photographer had hooked up with her for a couple of months but she hadn't really felt valued as a person; rather, she'd felt more of a commodity, a bit of arm candy to be paraded around to gain Brownie points with his colleagues. That relationship, as well as one or two others, had made her come to the conclusion that sex was something men *did* to her, rather than something she experienced *with* them. She had always been able to separate herself from the act, to keep her mind to one side, to be the impartial observer.

She had talked to girlfriends about it and they had assured her she just hadn't met the right partner. That it was all a matter of chemistry and timing. Animal attraction.

It was ironic that Angelique had one of the most looked-at bodies in the world, yet she felt a stranger to it in terms of passion. She knew how to pleasure herself but it wasn't something she did with any regularity. She didn't have the inclination or the desire. She wondered if she was just one of those people with little or no sex drive.

Remy's arm tightened across her middle and he nuzzled against the sensitive skin of her neck. 'Mmm…' he murmured sleepily.

The sex drive Angelique thought was non-existent suddenly made an appearance. It was centre-stage and wanted to be noticed. She felt it stir within her core, a tugging sensation, a needy little ache that wouldn't go away. Her breasts tingled from the brush of his arm as he shifted position again. His legs were entwined with hers and his erection—*his rock-hard erection*—was pressing against her thigh.

Was he even awake?

Maybe he was so practised at this he could do it in his sleep. She mentally rolled her eyes. It wouldn't surprise her.

One of his hands moved up and gently cupped the globe of her breast. Even through the satin of her nightie she felt his warmth and the electricity of his touch. It made her hungry for more, to feel that large, firm hand on her, skin to skin.

He rolled his thumb back and forth over her nipple, making it ache and tingle with pleasure.

OK, so he *had* to be awake.

The sensible part of Angelique knew this was the time to step in and remind him of the hands-off nature of their relationship, but the newly awakened *sensual* part of her was saying the opposite.

She wanted hands-on.

His mouth found the super-sensitive area just behind her earlobe. Angelique shivered as his tongue moved over the area in slow, lazy strokes. His hand moved up from her knee to the top of her thigh in one smooth caress that made her inner core clench tight with longing, triggering a rush of dewy moisture between her thighs.

He shifted position again, rolling her further on to her back as his body moved over hers.

You really should stop him.

Not yet! Not yet!

His hooded eyes slowly opened and then he flinched back from her as he let out a rather appropriate profanity. 'What the hell do you think you're doing?'

Angelique gave him a pointed look. 'What am *I* doing? You're the one with my breast in your hand.'

He frowned and looked down at his hand as if he had only just realised it was attached to his body and that he was the one with control over it. He dropped it from her and moved away and up off the bed.

He scraped the same hand through the thick black tousle of his hair and turned to glare at her. 'You should've woken me.'

She arched a brow. 'So you really *can* do it in your sleep.'

He gave her an irritated frown. 'Looks like you were running on automatic pilot as well. When were you going to call a halt?'

Some little demon inside Angelique decided it was time to rattle *his* cage for a change. She gave him a sultry look from beneath her lashes, her 1950s Hollywood movie-star look. 'Maybe I wasn't.'

A cynical look came into his eyes and his mouth hardened. 'It won't work, Angelique. I'm not staying married to you for a minute longer than I have to, so you can forget about your plans to snare yourself a rich husband. I'm not playing ball.'

She decided to press him a little further. *This was so much fun!* She had never seen him look quite so furious. His jaw was clenched and his hands were fisted. Where was his puerile sense of humour now? 'But you want me. You can hardly deny that.' She glanced at the tented fabric of his boxer shorts before giving him another smouldering smile.

His brows snapped together. 'You are *such* a piece of work. Is this how you hook your claws into every man who crosses your path?'

Angelique slowly stroked her right foot down over

her left ankle, her chest arched back as she rested on her elbows. 'You're hardly one to talk. Women run each other down to get into your bed. I didn't run to get here. I didn't even walk. I got here by default.'

'And now you're getting out of it.' He stepped forward and ripped the bed linen off her like a magician pulling a cloth from a table.

Angelique gave a startled squeal as he grabbed one of her ankles and tugged her towards him. 'Get your hands off me!'

'That's not what you were saying a minute ago.' He pulled her upright but she stumbled and would have fallen except for his arms coming around her to steady her.

She thought he would let her go but he didn't. If anything his firm grip on her hips tightened. She felt every imprint of his fingers pressing into her skin; she even wondered if they would leave marks.

She looked at his mouth, always a big mistake, but there you go. She couldn't seem to help herself. Her gaze was drawn like a tiny piece of metal to a powerful magnet.

Their bodies were touching, feeling, *discovering* each other's contours.

Angelique felt the heft, weight and heat of his erection pressing against her belly. It stirred her senses into a madcap frenzy of longing that took over her whole body. She felt the rush of heat from her core, the liquid of lust that was outside of her control.

'This is not what I want,' he ground out but still he didn't let her go.

'I don't want it either.' *You liar. You do want it. You want him.*

He suddenly put her from him, stepping back and

raking a hand through his hair again. 'OK… Let's get some time out here.'

Time out?

I want time in!

Angelique's little demon wasn't quite ready to back down. 'You're scared. You're worried you might get to like having me around, aren't you, Remy? You're not used to that feeling. You're the one who hires and fires your bedmates week by week. You don't form lasting attachments. You form convenient, casual alliances that temporarily scratch your itch.'

He glowered at her again. 'I do *not* want you around. You're nothing but trouble. You attract it and you revel in it. I don't want it.'

'Then give me back Tarrantloch and I'll be out of your life as soon as you can say blackjack.'

The silence vibrated with palpable tension.

'No.' His one-word answer was clipped and determined. *Very* determined. *Caffarelli* determined.

Angelique hitched up her chin. 'Then you're stuck with me. I'm not leaving your side until you give me what I want.'

'You don't want Tarrantloch.' His lip curled mockingly. 'What you want is a pat on the back from your father.'

'Ha ha,' she scoffed. 'And what *you* want is a big tick of approval from your grandfather. You think by taking possession of Tarrantloch that it will somehow win favour with him.'

He gave a harsh bark of laughter. 'I do not need my aging grandfather's approval to get on in life. I've made my own way. I don't need anyone's tick of approval to be happy.'

'You're not happy. That's why you're so restless. You

can't settle because you're not happy with who you are on the inside.' *Just like I'm not happy.*

His eyes flashed with ire. 'Oh, and you're an expert on that, are you? The woman who doesn't eat in case she puts on a gram of flesh. Don't make me laugh.'

Angelique hated that he knew so much about her, about her insecurities. How did he *do* that? They had barely seen each other for years, yet within such a short time he had summed her up in a sentence. 'I have a contract—'

'That insists you parade yourself in front of people who don't give a damn about you, to make millions of dollars for *them*. *You're* not important to them, only your body is. They don't want what's inside you, they're only interested in what they can get out of you.'

It was true.

It was painfully, agonizingly true.

It was a blunt truth she had come to acknowledge only very recently, which was why she was so keen to get out of the industry, to come at it from a different angle—the design and marketing angle.

But her confidence had always been the kicker and now it was even more so. She hadn't gone to university. She had no business degree or diploma. She hadn't even finished school. She had no official qualifications. What sort of ability did she have to run her own business?

She would be such a babe in the woods. It was cut-throat and dog-eat-dog out there. She had seen it first-hand. People with good intentions, with good skills and awesome talent were pushed aside by the power brokers, the money men who were only interested in the profit line.

'I'm not planning on modelling for too much longer.'

His gaze hardened. 'So am I part of the back-up

plan? The rich husband to bankroll your—' he made quotation marks with his fingers '—retirement plan?'

'I have my own designs.'

He looked at her for a moment in silence, a frown deepening across his forehead.

'Designs?'

Angelique let out a little breath. She had told no one about her plans. It seemed strange, almost ironic, she would be telling *him*. 'Not every woman is a size zero. There are women out there with post-baby bodies, with scars, who've had mastectomies, or with the track marks of age. None of us are perfect.'

'I can't believe you just said that.'

Her shoulders went down on a sigh. 'I'm tired of being the poster girl for perfection. It takes a lot of hard work to look this good.'

'You look pretty damn good.'

Angelique felt a frisson of delight at his comment. He *liked* the way she looked?

But it's not real.

If she ate properly she would be a size—maybe even two sizes—bigger. Would he—and the rest of the world—find her so attractive then?

She was a physical fraud.

And an even bigger emotional one.

Angelique hadn't been in touch with her emotions since the day she had stumbled across her mother's unconscious body when she was ten years old. She could still see the glass of water with the faint trace of her mother's lipstick around the rim.

The pill bottle that had been empty.

The silence.

Not even a heartbeat.

No pulse.

No mother.

Angelique had locked down her emotions and acted like a puppet ever since.

'I want to launch my own swim and leisurewear label. I've wanted to do it for a while. I want more control over my life and my career.'

'You'll need money to do that.'

'I know. I have some savings put aside, but it's not quite enough. I have do it properly or it will fold before it gets off the ground.'

'Is anyone offering to back you?'

'I've approached a couple of people but they were a little gun-shy.' She let out a little sigh. 'I think my reputation as a bit of a hell-raiser put them off.'

'How much of it is true?'

Angelique looked at him. 'The gun-shy people?'

'The hell-raising.'

Her shoulders went down in a little slump. 'I'm no angel…I've never tried to be. It's just the press make it out to be a hundred times worse than it is. I only have to be standing next to someone at a party or a nightclub or social gathering to be linked to them in some sort of salacious scandal.'

'You never defend yourself.' His expression was inscrutable, as if he was still making up his mind about her, whether to believe her or not. 'You've never asked for a retraction of any of the statements made about you.'

'What would be the point? Defensiveness only makes it worse.' She let out another sign. 'Anyway, to begin with I welcomed the gossip. I figured any publicity is good publicity. Some of the most famous models in the world are known for their behaviour as much as their looks.'

He rubbed a hand over his jaw. The raspy sound was loud in the silence. 'I have a couple of contacts who might be able to help you with launching your designs. I'd have to look at what you've got on the table first. I'm not going to recommend anything that hasn't got a chance of flying. I prefer to back winners, not losers.'

Angelique felt a little piqued that he didn't instantly believe in her. She hadn't realised until now how much she wanted him to have faith in her ability. To believe that she wasn't just another pretty face without any substance behind it. 'I wouldn't dream of putting your precious money at risk.' Her words were sharp, clipped with resentment.

He gave her a levelling look. 'I might love a gamble, Angelique, but at the end of the day I'm a businessman. I can't allow emotions to get in the way of a good business decision.'

She sent him a chilly glare. 'You didn't worry too much about your emotions when you tricked my father out of Tarrantloch. That wasn't a business decision. It was a personal vendetta and I'll never forgive you for it.'

'I admit I wanted to pay him back for what he did to my grandfather. We almost lost everything because of what he did.' His look was darkly scathing. 'But it wasn't just about that. I bet he didn't tell you the details of his underhand behaviour over the Ibiza account I was about to close? He would have put a completely different spin on it for his precious little girl.'

His precious little girl.

Angelique had to choke back a laugh. If only Remy knew how much her father despised her. He never showed it in public. He couldn't afford to tarnish his reputation as a devoted father. He put on a good show when the need arose but as soon as the doors were

closed Henri would revert back to his autocratic, boor-
ish, hyper-critical ways. She had always known her father had wanted a son as his firstborn but her mother
had failed to deliver one.

Angelique was a living, daily reminder of that failure.

'I know my father isn't a plaster saint but neither is
your grandfather,' she tossed back.

'I never said he was. I know how difficult he can be.'

She folded her arms across her chest. 'I don't want
your money, Remy. I want you to give me back what is
mine. That's all I want from you.'

'Not going to happen, *ma chérie*.' He gave her an intractable look. 'And, just for the record, I haven't finished with your father. Tarrantloch is nothing compared
to what he did to me in all but defaming me online. I'm
not stopping until I get the justice I want.'

Angelique curled her lip. 'Is that why you jumped
at the fiancée charade that led to this ridiculous marriage? You saw a perfect opportunity for revenge. For
rough justice. Forcing my hand in a marriage neither of
us wants in order to score points. That's so...*pathetic*
I want to throw up. '

His brows jammed together. 'Do you really think
I'd go that far? Come on, Angelique, you're not thinking straight. I don't want to be married to anyone, let
alone you. If by any remote chance I choose to settle
down with someone it won't be with someone like you.'

She gave him a huffy scowl. '*Like me?* What does
that mean? What's wrong with me?'

He let out a breath as he pushed a hand through his
hair. 'Nothing's wrong with you... It's just, I don't see
you as wife material.'

'Because?'

'Because you're not the "marriage and babies" type.'

Angelique raised her brows. 'You want...*babies*?'

He reared back from her as if she'd asked him if he wanted a deadly disease. 'No! God, no. I'm just saying...'

She gave him another scowl. 'I'm not sure what you're saying. Maybe you could elaborate a bit. Fill in the blanks for me.'

He looked about as flustered as she'd ever seen him. It was a rare sight. He was normally so in control—joking around. Having a laugh at everyone else's expense. Now he seemed to be back-pedalling as if he had stepped on a land mine and wasn't quite sure how to step off it without an explosion. 'It's not that I don't think you'd be a great mother.'

'But you think I'd be rubbish at being a wife.'

'I think you'd find it hard to compromise.'

Angelique blurted out a laugh. 'And *you* don't? Oh, for God's sake, Remy. You really are unbelievable. You're the least compromising person I've ever met. If I'd make a rotten wife, then you'd make an even worse husband.'

'Then thank God we'll be able to stop being a husband and wife as soon as we get back to England.'

'You really think it will be *that* simple?' Angelique asked. 'What if someone hears about this? A journalist or someone with contacts in the media? Did you see how many people were at our wedding? What if someone took a photo? What if *everyone* took a photo?'

His expression locked down, leaving just one muscle moving in and out on the left side of his jaw. 'No one is going to find out. We can annul this as soon as we land. I've already spoken to my lawyer in London. We can go straight to his office from the airport. It will be over and we can both move on with our lives as if it never happened.'

Good luck with that, Angelique thought. She'd been lucky lately in keeping her face out of the gossip pages but she knew it wouldn't last. If a journalist got a whiff of what had happened in Dharbiri she and Remy would be besieged by the media as soon as they landed. But then, anyone with a camera phone could snap a picture of them together and email or text it to a newspaper.

Even arriving at Heathrow together was going to cause a stir because there were always people coming back from holidays from tropical locations where her body had been on yet another billboard.

Oh joy…

CHAPTER SIX

REMY COULD NOT believe the sort of attention Angelique attracted. Even before they had cleared Customs people were nudging each other and pointing. Several came up and asked for autographs. Some took photos, even though the signs in the customs area strictly forbade the use of phones or cameras.

'Do you have to be so damn nice to everybody?' he said in a low, gruff tone as he ushered her through to where a driver was waiting to collect them. 'Can't you pretend you're not you? Let them think they've got the wrong person or something. I've done that heaps of times. It works like a charm.'

'*You've* got the wrong person if you think I'd be rude to someone who paid a lot of money for a swimsuit I've modelled.' She smiled at another fan who came over with a pen and a boarding pass for her to sign.

Remy could feel his blood pressure rising. Was she doing this on purpose? People were looking at *him* now, trying to figure out who he was and how he fitted into her life. How long before they recognised him and put two and two together?

He took her firmly by the elbow. 'We have to go. *Now.*'

'Hold your horses.' She winked up at him cheekily. 'Or your camels.'

She smiled again as yet another person came over and told her how much they admired her, and that they didn't believe for a second all that rubbish about her and the English banker who was married, and how it wasn't her fault the marriage had broken up because it was obviously doomed from the outset, blah, blah, blah.

Remy had to wait until they were in the car before he asked, 'Did you know the banker was married when you hooked up with him?'

'I didn't hook up with him.' She flicked some imaginary lint off her clothing. 'I was photographed next to him in a hotel lobby. I was waiting for the porter to bring out my luggage.'

He frowned at her. 'Are you seriously telling me you didn't have anything to do with him? That you didn't have a secret love tryst with him in that hotel?'

She gave him a bored look. 'Does every woman you speak to end up sharing your bed?' She held up her hand and gave her eyes a little roll. 'No, don't answer that. I already know. If they're under the age of thirty, they probably do.'

'I don't do married women. I might be a playboy but I do have *some* standards.'

'Good to know.' There was something about her tone and the exaggerated way she inspected her perfectly manicured nails that irked him.

'What do you mean?'

'It's very reassuring, that's all.'

He frowned again. He could sense she was up to something. 'What is?'

'That you don't *do* married women.'

'Why's that?'

Her look was arch when she turned to look at him.
'Because I'm married.'

A surge of hot, unbridled lust rose in his loins. He
could not think of a woman he wanted more than her
right now. It was pounding through him like an unstoppable tide. It tapped into every thread of desire he had
ever felt for her, thickening it, swelling it, *reinforcing* it.

He covered it with a laugh. 'But not for much longer.'

She put her chin in the air and inspected her nails
again. 'That annulment can't happen soon enough.' She
lowered her hand back down to her lap and studied it
for a moment. 'I can't think of a worse forty-eight hours
in my life.'

'Hell of a short marriage,' he said after a little pause.
'Do you think that's some sort of record?'

She shrugged one of her slim shoulders a little without looking at him. 'Maybe.'

Another silence.

'Are you heading back to Paris after this?' Remy
asked. 'This' being the sign-off of their brief marriage.
He didn't want to admit it but he would miss her. A bit.
A niggly bit. She was incredibly annoying but vastly
entertaining. He could think of worse things to do with
his time than spar with her. She stimulated him physically and intellectually. Not many women did that.

In fact, he couldn't think of the last one that had…

'I have a shoot in Barbados.' Her shoulders went
down dejectedly. 'I have to lose at least three pounds
before then.'

'You're joking, surely?'

She gave him a resigned look. 'No one wants to see
a bloated belly in a bikini they're going to pay a hundred and fifty pounds for, are they?'

'But you've got an amazing belly.' He'd been having

shower fantasies about it for years. He compared other women to her. He knew it was wrong but he couldn't help it. She was his benchmark. That billboard in New York all those years ago had nailed it for him. No one even came close.

He suddenly found himself imagining her belly swelling…growing larger with the bloom of a child… *his* child…

Whoa! What are you thinking?

She pressed her lips together. 'I've got a belly like every other woman. It has its good days and its bad days.'

Remy studied her for a moment. 'Is that why you don't eat?'

She visibly bristled. 'I *do* eat.'

He gave a disparaging grunt. 'Not enough to keep a gnat alive.'

She sent him a flinty glare. 'So you keep a catalogue of all your lovers' food intakes, do you?'

'You're not my lover.' A fact his body was reminding him of virtually non-stop. Why wasn't it letting up?

'No.' Her chin hitched up until she was eyeball to eyeball with him. 'I'm just your wife.'

Remy felt his back come up at the way she said the word. It was like she was spitting out a nasty object, something foul and distasteful. 'Why are you so against being a wife? Your parents were happily married, weren't they? Everyone said how devastated your father was when your mother died. He was inconsolable.'

'Yes, he was…' Her expression clouded and her teeth nipped into her bottom lip.

He wondered if he should have mentioned her mother's death. Suicide was a touchy subject. Kate March-and had taken an overdose after a bout of depression, which had supposedly been accidental, and rumour had it Angelique had found her body.

She had been ten years old.

The same age his brother Rafe had been when their parents had been killed.

Remy had seen first-hand what a child with an over-blown sense of responsibility went through. It had only been since Rafe had met Poppy that he had let that sense of responsibility ease. Rafe had taken stock of his life and was a better and happier man for it.

Raoul had done much the same, recognising his life would not be complete without Lily Archer, the woman who had shown him that physical wholeness was not as important as emotional wholeness.

But what could Angelique teach Remy other than patience and self-control?

Remy wondered if finding her mother like that was why she was such a tearaway. Losing her mother in such a way must have hit her hard. Had she blamed herself?

He looked at her sitting with her arms folded across her middle, her gaze focused on the tote bag on her lap. A frown was pulling on her forehead and her teeth were savaging her lower lip. She looked far younger than her years. Vulnerable.

'Did you blame yourself for your mother's death?'

'A bit, I suppose. What child wouldn't?' She started plucking at the stitches in the leather of her bag strap, tugging at the tiny threads as if to unpick them one by one. 'If I'd got home earlier I might've been able to save her. But I'd stopped at a friend's house on the way home from school. I'd never done that before.' She stopped picking to look at him. 'Needless to say, I never did it again.'

There was a lot of pain in her eyes. She covered it

well but it was there lurking in the depths. Remy saw it in the way she held herself, a braced posture, guarded, prepared. Vigilant. There was so much about her that annoyed him, yet how much of that was a ruse to cover her true nature? Her brash wilfulness, her impulsiveness, her refusal to obey instructions could well be a shield to hide how vulnerable and alone she felt.

'Monsieur Caffarelli?'

Remy had almost forgotten they were still in the car until it came to a halt and the driver opened the partition that separated the driver from the passengers.

'There are paparazzi outside,' his driver said. 'Do you want me to drive another block or two?'

'Yes, do that.' Remy took out his phone. 'I'll give my lawyer a call to see if he can meet us somewhere else.'

'How did they know we were going to your lawyer's office?' Angelique asked.

'God knows.' He put his phone to his ear. 'Brad. You looked out of your window lately?'

'I was just about to call you,' Brad said. 'I've just had Robert Mappleton on the line. He heard a rumour you're married to Henri Marchand's daughter and—'

'Where the hell did he hear that?' Remy barked.

'Not sure,' Brad said. 'Maybe someone in Dharbiri spoke to the press. All I know is this is like winning the lottery for you right now.'

'What are you talking about?' Remy said.

'Have you forgotten? You've been trying to win this guy over for months. *The* Bob Mappleton of Mappleton Hotels?'

'That crusty old bastard who refused to even discuss a takeover bid, even though the shareholders are threatening to call in the administrators?' Remy curled his lip. *All because of that inflammatory email Henri March-*

and had circulated. 'Yeah, how could I forget? He'd rather face total bankruptcy than strike a deal with me.'

'Well, here's the thing,' Brad said. 'He just called and said he's changed his mind. He wasn't prepared to do business with a hard-partying playboy, but now you're married to Henri Marchand's daughter he figures that stuff Marchand said about you last year can't have been true. He wants to set up a meeting. He's as old-school and conservative as they come but this marriage of yours couldn't have come at a better time.'

Remy felt his scalp start to tingle. The biggest take-over bid of his career: a chain of run-down hotels he knew he could make into the most luxurious and popular in the world. The Ibiza development was child's play compared to this.

The catch?

He had to stay married in order to nail it.

He looked at Angelique who was giving him the evil eye. He could see the storm brewing in her grey-blue eyes. He could feel the air tightening along with her body. Every muscle in her face had turned to stone. 'Call him and set up a meeting for the end of next week,' he said to Brad.

'Why next week? Why not this week? Why not today?' Brad asked.

Remy grinned. 'Because I'm going on my honeymoon.' And then he closed his phone and started counting.

One.

Two...

'What?' Angelique spluttered. 'I'm not staying married to you!'

'Has anyone ever told you how cute you look when you're angry?'

Her eyes iced and narrowed, her voice coming out through clenched teeth. 'Don't try your charm on me, Remy Caffarelli. It won't work. I'm not staying married to you, so you can just call your lawyer right back and tell him we'll be up there in a less than a minute to sign on the dotted—'

'What if you were to get something out of it?'

Her head slanted at a suspicious angle. 'Such as?'

'I'll back your label,' Remy said. 'With my connections and guaranteed finance you could really take your designs places. You'll become a global brand overnight.'

She wavered like a wary dog being offered a treat from someone it didn't quite trust. 'How long would we have to stay married?'

He gave a shrug. 'A couple of months tops. We can get the wheels rolling on our business ventures and then call it quits. Easy.'

'It's still going to be a paper marriage, right?'

Remy found himself wondering if he could tweak the rules a tad. Just a tad, mind. A couple of months with Angelique in his bed could certainly make the temporary sacrifice of his freedom worthwhile.

Besides, it wasn't as if he could sleep with anyone else while he was officially married to her. It went against everything he believed in.

'That would depend.'

'On what?'

'On whether you wanted to be celibate for two months or whether you wanted a paper marriage with benefits,' he said.

An insolent spark lit her gaze. 'Is that the only choice I have? Celibacy or you?'

Remy gave her a winning smile. 'I know; it's a tough one. But wait. There's more. I'll set up a business plan and employ accounting staff to see to the details while you get on with designing and sourcing fabrics.' It was like reeling a fish on the line. He could practically see her mouth watering. *He was going to win this.*

'It's not enough.'

He frowned. 'What do you mean, it's not enough? I'm the one taking a risk here. I haven't even seen one of your designs. You could be rubbish at designing for all I know.'

Her small chin came up. 'I want more.'

More what? Money? Sex? He could tick both those boxes several times over. 'I won't sleep around on you, if that's what's worrying you,' Remy said. 'I'm a one-at-a-time man and I'd expect the same commitment from you. I won't settle for anything else.'

Her eyes held his a challenging little lockdown that made the base of his spine shift like sand moving in an hourglass. 'I'm not going to sleep with you, Remy.'

Sure you're not, Remy thought. He could feel her attraction for him ringing in the air like a high-pitched radio frequency. She wanted him but she didn't want to be the first one to give in to it.

He saw it in those looks she gave him when she thought he wasn't looking: hungry, yearning, lustful. She was proud and defiant, determined to withstand the temptation he was dangling before her.

He was used to women caving in to his first smile. Angelique's resistance to his charm was doing the opposite of what she probably intended. Instead of making him want her less, it made him want her more. She was a challenge. A goal to score. A prize to claim.

A bet to win.

'Do you want to put money on that?' he asked.

She gave him a mordant look. 'Thanks, but no.'

'You're definitely not your father's daughter.'

'Ah, but that's where you're wrong,' she said, still eyeballing him with those stormcloud eyes.

Remy could feel his desire for her thundering through his blood. How he loved a woman with spirit, and they didn't come much more spirited than Angelique. He would relish every single moment of having her finally succumb to him. The chase would be fun but the catch would be magnificent. He could already taste the victory. He could feel it in his blood and in his bones.

He would have her.

He would have her right where he had always secretly wanted her.

In his bed.

Her beautiful face was held at a regal height, her eyes glittering with an implacable purpose. 'I think you'll find I'm very much my father's daughter.'

'Because you don't know when to quit when failure is staring you in the face?' He gave an amused chuckle. 'That would certainly be a case of the apple not falling far from the tree.'

Her chin stayed at that haughty level, her mouth set in a tight line. 'I'll stay married to you on one condition and one condition only.'

Remy felt a warning tingle course through his blood; even the back of his neck started to prickle. 'Go on.'

The corner of her mouth lifted as if she knew she had this in the bag. 'I want Tarrantloch at the end of it.'

CHAPTER SEVEN

REMY DREW IN a breath. Why couldn't she want a life-long stipend or a bank vault of diamonds? But no, not Angelique; instead she had insisted on the one thing he didn't want to relinquish. Would *never* relinquish.

Tarrantloch was a trophy. He wasn't prepared to hand it over before he'd enjoyed everything it represented: *success. Revenge. Justice.*

He leaned forward to give the driver instructions to take him to his regular hotel in Paddington. He wanted time to plan a counter-move. He wasn't going to let her manipulate him. His mind shuffled through the ways he could turn this to his advantage. She didn't want the property half as much as she wanted to beat him at his own game. This was another one of her power plays.

'You drive a hard bargain,' he said when he sat back again.

She acknowledged that with an aristocratic tilt of her head. 'You want me to be your wife? That's the price you have to pay.'

Remy knew he could turn this around. Easily. Besides, she had got under his skin with her haughty airs and don't-touch-me looks.

He knew she wanted him.

It was in the air between them every time they were

alone. It had been there for years, truth be told. Now he could act on the desire he had always suppressed for her. He could finally indulge his senses, binge on her body until she was out of his system and out of his head. It would not be much of a hardship spending a month or two with her in a red-hot affair. He would be the envy of every man with a pulse.

Remy smiled a secret smile. He would be the one to finally tame the temptress, the wild and sultry Angelique Marchand.

'I don't know…' He rubbed at his jaw as if thinking it over. 'Tarrantloch for a couple of months of pretence? Doesn't seem fair to me.'

'*Fair?*' she shot back incredulously. 'Of course it's fair. I never wanted to be anyone's wife either, for real or pretend. It will just about kill me to spend two months acting like I feel something for you other than loathing.'

Remy had never wanted to make her eat those words more than at that moment. She didn't hate him as much as she made out. She hated that he saw through her game-playing and manipulative attempts to outsmart him.

But he would *always* win.

Losing was not an option for him.

'Like you, I want more.'

Her eyes suddenly flared. 'How much more?'

He gave her a smouldering look. 'I think you know how much more.'

She tried to disguise a swallow. 'You're joking.'

'It's a big house,' he said. 'I put a lot at risk to acquire it. I'm not going to relinquish it unless I think it's well and truly worth it.'

She gave him a gimlet glare. 'I think I should've faced the gallows or the firing squad or a public flogging back in that godforsaken place we just left. It would've been preferable to this…this *outrageous* proposition of yours.'

Remy laid his arm along the back of her seat, his fingers close enough to touch the nape of her neck. 'What's so outrageous about making love with someone you've desired for years?'

'I don't desire you. I've *never* desired you.' Her eyes flashed pure venom at him. 'I detest you.'

He caught a coil of her hair and tethered her to him. He watched as her grey-blue eyes flared and her tongue swept over her lips again. 'I could make you eat those words, *ma belle.*'

Her mouth was pinched tight. 'You can't make me eat anything.'

There was something incredibly arousing about her defiant stance. She pulled against his push. She had always stood up to him. Challenged him. Annoyed him. Goaded him. 'I'll have you eating out of my hand soon enough.' He gave her a confident smile. 'You won't be able to resist.'

She grabbed her hair and tugged it out of his hold even though it must have hurt. 'I hate you for this.'

He gave a negligent shrug. 'So what's new?'

Her eyes narrowed to slits. 'I mean I'll *really* hate you.'

'So.' He curled his lip mockingly. 'You've only been pretending up until now?'

'I can't believe you're being so ruthless about this.' She continued to glare at him. 'You don't want me at all. You just want to win the upper hand.'

He caught her hand and brought it to his groin, holding it against his throbbing heat. 'Oh, I want you all right, princess,' he drawled. 'Make no mistake about that. And what I want, I get. Every. Single. Time.'

She snatched her hand back and glowered at him. 'Then you've met your match, Remy Caffarelli, because I bend my will to no man. If you want to sleep with me, then you'll have to tie me to the bed first.'

Remy smiled a sinful smile. 'I can hardly wait.'

Angelique seethed as she waited for him to come round to open her door when they arrived at his hotel. The press must have been given a tip-off as they surged towards him, but he just gave them one of his butter-wouldn't-melt smiles.

'Mr Caffarelli, the news of your marriage to Angelique Marchand has surprised everyone. Have you any comment to make on your whirlwind relationship?'

'No comment other than to say I haven't even told my family about it yet.' Remy grinned at the television camera. 'Rafe, Raoul, if you're watching this—sorry I didn't tell you guys first. You too, *Nonno*. Bet you didn't see that coming. But I wanted to surprise you all. Who would have thought it? Me, head over heels in love.'

Angelique mentally rolled her eyes as Remy helped her out of the car. 'Do you have to be so…?'

'Smile for the cameras, *ma chérie*,' he said as he took her by the hand in a firm, almost crushing grip.

'But I—'

'Miss Marchand.' A journalist thrust a recording device at her. 'Your marriage to Remy Caffarelli is the biggest scoop our network has had in decades. There are photos going viral with you in that gorgeous, ancient wedding dress. Can you tell us about your secret wedding?'

'It was very romantic,' Remy said before Angelique

could answer. 'Very traditional too, wasn't it, *mon amour*?'

'Very.' Angelique stretched her mouth into a smile. 'In fact, you would not believe quite *how* traditional it—'

Remy pulled her tightly against his shoulder. 'Right, show's over, folks. We've got things to do.'

'Miss Marchand, there's been some speculation going around on whether or not Remy has followed the example of his older brothers in not making his bride sign a pre-nuptial agreement. That's surprising, given the Caffarellis' wealth. Is that true in your case?'

Angelique felt Remy's hold on her tighten to the point of pain. But then he seemed to force himself to relax, although she could still feel the tension in him as he stood with his arm loosely around her shoulders. 'Yes, that's true,' she said in dulcet tones. Two could play at this game. 'It just goes to show how much he loves and trusts me.'

'Will you show us your rings?' a female journalist said.

'No rings as yet,' Remy said. 'We're still waiting for them to be finished. I'm afraid I didn't give the designer enough notice.'

Angelique looked up at him with feigned affection. 'It was an impulsive, spur-of-the-moment proposal, wasn't it, *mon cher*? You just couldn't hold it in any longer, could you?'

His dark-brown eyes warned her she would be paying for this later but right now Angelique didn't care. 'That's right,' he said. 'I couldn't wait to make her my wife. Now, if you'll excuse us…'

'One last question, Miss Marchand,' the female journalist said. 'Does your marriage to Remy Caffarelli mean there is now an end to the bitter feud between your father and Remy's grandfather, or are you star-crossed lovers?'

'Um…'

'I'm sure Henri Marchand will be thrilled to know his daughter has married a man who worships the ground she walks on,' Remy said smoothly.

'So you didn't ask his permission, then?' the female journalist asked with a cheeky smile.

Remy gave the journalist a level look. 'I did not believe that was necessary. Angelique is an adult and does not need her father's permission to do anything, much less marry the man she has loved since she was a teenager.'

'Is that true, Miss Marchand?' The journalist swung the recording device back to Angelique. 'Have you been in love with Remy since you were a girl?'

Angelique felt her teeth grind together behind her smile. 'Absolutely. Head over heels. Besotted. Totally, utterly smitten.'

Remy held up a hand to field off further questions. 'That's all, folks. No further comment.'

He practically dragged her into the building with him. 'Hey, not so fast,' Angelique said, almost stumbling over the pavement. 'I'm wearing heels.'

He slowed his pace but his grip on her hand didn't loosen. 'Behave yourself, Angelique, or you might find your time with me unnecessarily unpleasant.'

She threw him a caustic look. 'More than it is already?'

His expression was deceptively cool and composed but she knew she had riled him to the edge of his control. She felt it in the tense grip of his fingers. 'If you want to get your way at the end of this then you'll have to play the part of the happy bride, especially in public. Do you understand?'

'So, you agree to give me Tarrantloch?'

A steely glint came into his eyes. 'We'll see.'

Angelique narrowed her gaze in anger. 'If you don't give me a straight yes or no then I'm going to walk back out there and tell those journalists this is nothing but a sham.'

His hold on her wrist tightened like a vice. 'You're not going anywhere, young lady. For once in your life, you're going to do as you're told. That will make a refreshing change for you, *n'est-ce pas*?'

'Welcome back, Mr Caffarelli,' the hotel manager said as he came over to shake Remy's hand. 'A little bird tells me congratulations are in order. On behalf of all of us here, may I wish you both a very happy future together.'

'*Merci,*' Remy said with a polished smile.

Angelique had to bite her tongue not to blurt out the truth but she knew in the end she would be the one to look foolish. Remy had a knack for turning things to his advantage. Didn't the last twenty-four hours prove it? He was going to make the most of being married to her.

Damn him!

'How long are you staying with us?' the manager asked.

'Just tonight,' Remy said. 'We'll be moving on first thing in the morning. If you could keep the press away from us, I would greatly appreciate it, Thomas.'

'Will do, sir.' Thomas beamed. 'We took the liberty of preparing the bridal suite for you.'

Not another one!

'That was indeed very kind of you,' Remy said with a glinting smile. 'I'll make sure we do it justice.'

Angelique had to wait until they were in the lift and alone before she could give him a piece of her mind. 'I can't believe you said that. Now they'll be sniggering down there imagining us up here doing…it.'

He hooked a dark brow upwards. 'It?'

She folded her arms and glowered at him. 'I bet it's a pretty regular occurrence, you bringing scores of women upstairs to have sex with them.'

'Never in the bridal suite, however, and only one at a time.'

She flickered her eyelids in disgust. 'You're unbelievable.'

The lift doors pinged open and he waved for her to go ahead of him. 'Jealous, *ma belle*?'

Angelique made a rude vomiting noise as she breezed past him. 'You have *got* to be joking.'

He opened the suite door but blocked the entrance with his body. 'This is the fun part.'

'Pardon?'

He held out his arms. 'I get to carry you over the threshold.'

Angelique backed away. 'Oh, no you don't. You're not putting your hands anywhere on me—

'*Hey!* What are you doing? *Put me down this instant!*'

Remy's arms were like steel cables around her as they carried her into the suite. Angelique kicked her legs and pummelled his chest with her fists but it was like a goldfish trying to fight off a tiger shark. 'Is that the best you can do?' he taunted as he kicked the door shut with his foot.

Angelique grabbed a fistful of his hair and pulled. *Hard*. 'I'm just starting, so don't say I didn't warn you.'

He slid her down the entire length of his rock-hard

body, leaving her in no doubt of his red-hot desire for her. 'So am I,' he drawled and covered her mouth with the blistering heat of his.

It was a hard kiss, an almost crushing one, but it stirred an ember inside Angelique into a suddenly combustible flame. It didn't matter that she was supposed to be fighting him off for the sake of her pride. All that was important now was keeping his mouth locked on hers as her senses spun, twirled and reeled in delight.

His hands were rough as they gripped her by the hips, his erection heavy and urgent against her feminine mound. She felt the tug and drag of desire deep and low in her belly, that restless urge to be closer to him, to be possessed by his thick, hot length, was almost unbearable.

Every lustful thought or dream she'd had about him was making her giddy with the anticipation of finally experiencing his possession. Was that why she had continued to niggle and goad him—to push his buttons? To make him lose control and do what they had always wanted to do to each other even though, if asked, both would have flatly denied it?

She kissed him back with primal heat, using her teeth and her tongue, her hands still tightly fisted in his hair, her breasts jammed up against his chest, making her nipples ache and tingle as they were abraded by the fabric of his shirt.

His tongue duelled with hers until she was making needy, hungry little whimpering noises in the back of her throat. One of his hands went to the zip at the back of her dress and lowered it in one swift but smooth slide, his warm hand cupping her bottom through the cobweb lace of her knickers as he pulled her even closer to his turgid length.

An inferno seemed to be raging inside her body. It was lighting spot fires all over her flesh, burning her, searing her with the need to feel him skin on skin.

'Damn you,' he growled against her lips, making them vibrate with lust.

She tugged at his lower lip with her teeth, tasting blood but not sure if it was hers or his. 'Damn you right back.'

He sucked in a breath and crushed his mouth to hers again, harder this time, going deeper with his tongue until no corner of her mouth was undiscovered. He was consuming her like a hungry man does a feast and she was doing exactly the same. He was a sensual banquet she couldn't resist. Would she ever have enough of his mouth, of his electrifying touch?

His hands shoved her dress away from her shoulders, letting it puddle at her feet. He unhooked her bra and cupped her right breast in his hand as his other kept her locked against his pulsing heat. His thumb moved over her tight nipple in a mesmerising back-and-forth motion that made her spine loosen like oil poured into a rusty lock.

Angelique slid a hand between their bodies so she could unzip him. Ever since that shocking moment in the car when he'd pushed her hand against him, her palm had been tingling to feel him without the barrier of clothes.

He groaned with approval against her mouth as she freed him from his underwear. She shaped him with her fingers first, getting to know the feel, length and weight of him. Then she started rubbing up and down his silky shaft, registering every guttural sound he made, delighting in every flinch or movement of pleasure he made. She felt the beading of his pre-ejaculatory moisture and rolled it around the head of his penis, inciting him, urging him on. Daring him. Wanting him. Aching for him.

He was on his own sensual mission to get her naked. Her knickers were soon dispensed with and she had barely stepped away from the tiny circle of them when his fingers found her hot wetness. She gasped as he slipped them inside her; it was the sweetest torture to have him but not have him quite the way she wanted him. She moved against the blissful friction, making throaty little pleas against his plundering mouth.

'Condom.' The word sounded like it was wrung out of him.

'Have you got one?' *Dumb question.* He probably had hundreds on him. Maybe even thousands. He probably had his own insignia on them.

'In my back pocket.' He walked her backwards further into the suite, his mouth still fused to hers as his hand searched for the protection in the pocket of his jeans.

Angelique took the foil packet off him and saw to the business end of things. She tried not to fumble in her haste but her hands were shaking in anticipation. For most of her adult life she had dreamed and fantasised about feeling this level of lust.

It was overpowering.

Totally consuming.

Unstoppable.

It was as if every nerve in her body was standing up on its tiptoes and screaming out for release. *Now! Now! Now!*

It made every single encounter she had had—not that there had been many—pale in comparison.

'You are so damn hot and wet and ready for me,' he

said as he tumbled with her onto the king-sized bed in a sexy tangle of limbs.

'Yes.' One word was all she could manage. Her heart was racing, her blood pumping and her flesh tingling as he came over her with his weight.

He hitched up one of her legs over his hip and entered her so deeply she cried out as his thickened flesh stretched hers to capacity. He immediately stilled and looked down at her with a frown knitting his brows together. 'Am I rushing you?'

Angelique let out a little breath. 'No… Sorry, I'm a bit out of practice. It's been a while.'

His dark eyes searched hers. 'How long?'

'A few weeks… Months…'

His gaze was still locked on hers. 'Months?'

'OK, a year…and a bit. Two, actually…'

'But the press…'

'Get it wrong occasionally.'

His frown was still tugging at his forehead like stitches being pulled beneath the skin. 'Why do you let people say all that stuff about you when it isn't true?'

Angelique stroked a finger down his sternum, focusing on its journey rather than staying connected with his gaze. 'I don't care what people think. I know what's true. That's all that matters to me.'

'Stop distracting me.' He captured her hand and held it firmly in the cage of his. 'I want to talk to you.'

She couldn't help an exaggerated little eye-roll. 'I bet that's what you say to all the girls.'

His frown deepened. 'Will you stop it, for God's sake? I'm trying to have a sensible conversation with you.'

'While your body is doing what it's doing to mine?' Angelique writhed beneath him. 'Can't you feel that?'

He bit back a curse and moved within her. Deeply. Roughly. Urgently. 'I can't stop myself from wanting you. I hate myself for it.'

She grabbed at his buttocks and dug her fingers in to hold him in place. 'I hate myself for it too. I hate *you* for it. For how you make me feel.'

His mouth curved in an indolent smile. 'How do I make you feel?'

She tried to glare at him but it didn't quite work with his body still intimately connected with hers. Instead, she pushed out her bottom lip in a pout. 'Mad.'

'I like it when you're mad at me.' He gave one slow, deep thrust. 'It turns me on.'

Angelique felt her belly do a funny little shuffle like the pages of a book being thumbed. Her body was fully aware of him. Excruciatingly so. Every nerve ending was primed for his next thrust. She felt the tension building in her flesh with every erotic movement of his body in hers. He increased the pace and her pleasure rapidly climbed with the pulsating throb of her swollen, sensitised tissues as they each clamoured for release.

He hitched her leg higher over his hip and drove even deeper.

It was like detonating an explosive device.

Angelique felt the explosion deep in her body, radiating out in pulsing waves that ricocheted through her. She shuddered and screamed, a raw, primal-sounding scream that was unlike any other sound she had ever made before. But then she had never felt anything like this before either. She bucked beneath his rocking body to keep the exquisite sensations going for as long as she could. Finally they faded and she was left in a blissful state of lassitude.

But he wasn't finished with her yet.

He shifted position slightly, slowing his pace until her body was crawling with need once more. She felt the tingling start all over again, the tightening of muscles, the pulse of longing and the steady climb to the summit that was tantalisingly just out of reach.

He slipped a hand underneath her buttocks and raised her as he thrust deeper and faster. She looked at his face, at the taut set to his features as he fought for control. His eyes were hooded, his jaw like honed steel, his breathing sounding harsh and laboured. She had never seen a more erotic sight. A beautifully cut and carved man in full arousal, poised to explode, waiting for that final trigger.

Angelique lifted and then rolled her hips. He grimaced as he tried to hold back but then she rolled her pelvis again. She felt the exact moment when his control slipped. He stiffened and then let out a shout, the pumping action of his body triggering another wave of pleasure through her body that travelled all the way to her fingertips and toes.

He slumped over her, burying his head to the side of her neck, his warm breath and stubbly skin a deliciously sensual caress against hers.

Angelique was so used to sparring with him that this new connectedness was faintly disturbing. If he could read her body so well, how well could he read her mind?

She wasn't used to feeling such powerful sensations during sex. She had never felt that level of desire or need before. She had never orgasmed with a partner before. She'd always pretended and got away with it.

This was so new and exciting. Breathtaking. Tantalising. Addictive.

Dangerous.

Remy finally lifted his head and looked at her. 'Was that good for you?'

His arrogant confidence made her retort 'Average.'

His brown eyes glinted as if he knew she was lying. 'Then maybe I should try and improve my rating.' He stroked a lazy finger down between her breasts where a tiny slick of sweat had pooled. 'You're incredibly beautiful.'

She gave him one of her bored looks. 'Do you know how many times I've heard that?'

His eyes tethered hers; dark, probing, penetrating. 'Ah, but do you believe it?'

Angelique felt as if he had already cracked open a corner of her mind and was examining the contents with a high-beam searchlight. She put her hands on his chest and pushed him away. 'I have to get up. I don't want the condom to leak.'

He got up and dealt with the disposal of the condom while she went in search of her clothes. She felt foolish and somehow sordid, scrabbling about the room, picking up her underwear and redressing while all he had to do was straighten his clothes and zip up his trousers.

Was it somehow indicative of the imbalance of their relationship? She would always be the one who felt naked and exposed while he would only reveal what he wanted her to see.

He was in control.

She wasn't.

'Is this yours?' Remy asked, holding up a diamond pendant swinging on a fine gold chain.

Angelique went to take it off him but he held it just out of her reach. 'Give it to me.'

His mouth was curved in a sarcastic smile. 'Where are your manners, *mon amour*?'

She ground her teeth and flashed him a resentful look. 'Please.'

'Not good enough.' He held the pendant higher as she took another swipe at it. 'I want to hear you ask nicely.'

She felt a ripple of annoyance course through her, tightening every muscle to snapping point. 'Give it to me, *please*.'

His chocolate-brown eyes contained a goading glint. 'You can do better than that, *ma belle*. I want to hear you beg.'

Angelique felt the sudden rush of her fury as it unleashed itself from the tight restraints she had spent a lifetime keeping in place.

She would *not* beg.

She would *not* plead.

She would *not* give in to his command like a servant who had no rights. She would scratch his eyes out before she did that.

She flew at him like a dervish, calling him every foul name she could think of. It all came bubbling out like poison—the rage, the hatred, the feeling of impotence, the shame at being under his control when she had worked so hard not be under any man's control.

He had subdued her sensually.

He had ambushed her.

Disarmed her.

Now he wanted to break her spirit just like her father had done to her mother.

Of course, she was no match for him. He took control of her flailing fists before they could even land a punch. 'What the hell is wrong with you?' he asked, frowning at her.

Angelique pulled against his iron-like hold. 'Let go of me, you…you *bastard*!'

'Not until you simmer down.' His tone was calm but implacable. 'You're going to hurt yourself carrying on like that. What's got into you?'

Tears started and burned in her eyes. It was the greatest shame of all to be snivelling like a child in front of him but there was nothing she could do to stop the flow once it had started. She choked back a sob but another one soon followed, and then another, and another until she finally bowed her head and gave in to the storm of weeping. It was lowering to find herself in such a vulnerable state. How could she have let this happen? What was wrong with her? Where was her pride and determination? Had his powerful love-making undone her completely? How would she get herself together again?

Remy released her wrists but he gathered her to him, putting his arms around her so the wall of his body supported her. One of his hands went to the back of her head and gently stroked her hair as she shook with sobs against him. 'I've upset you.' His voice was very deep and sounded surprised. Perhaps even a little shocked.

Angelique gave an almighty sniff, and as if by magic a neatly folded white handkerchief with an embroidered black *C* on it was handed to her. 'Thanks.'

'Don't mention it.'

She blew her nose and scrunched the handkerchief into a ball inside her hand. 'I'm fine now.' She took a ragged breath and glanced up at him with an attempt at wryness. 'Bet you don't think I'm so beautiful now.'

His expression was clouded with concern as he looked down at her. 'I was only teasing. You do know that, don't you, *ma petite*?'

Why did he have to keep calling her those wonderful endearments in that sexy accent of his? It made it so much harder to hate him.

You don't hate him.

Angelique skirted around the thought and gave him a small self-deprecating smile. 'It's a bit of a hot button for me. A red rag, if you like. I don't beg. Ever. For anything.'

'I'll make a note of it.'

The silence thrummed for a moment.

She tucked a tendril of hair back behind her ear. 'Um…I guess I should go and clean up.'

He handed her the pendant, his expression now inscrutable. 'It's very nice. Was it a gift from one of your lovers?'

The fine chain tickled Angelique's palm as it coiled there. 'It was my mother's.' She raised her chin a fraction. 'Just for the record, I don't accept gifts from my lovers. Ever.'

He held her gaze for a beat or two, his still dark and unfathomable. 'Apart from Scottish mansions, of course.'

She pursed her lips at his counter-move. Would he end up giving her back Tarrantloch? He hadn't made any promises. Nothing was written down or signed. They had consummated their relationship, but did that mean anything to him other than yet another sexual conquest?

Angelique gave a little shrug of her shoulder as if it didn't matter to her either way. 'I'm sure you'll do the right thing when it comes to the end of our relationship.' She met his gaze again with a bold look. 'Have you got a date in mind or are we just going to wing it?'

The screen was still down over his eyes but a tiny muscle tightened near his mouth. 'Don't worry. I'll give you plenty of notice.'

She smiled a saccharine-sweet smile. 'Big of you.'

He let out an audible breath. 'You have first shower. I have some things to see to. We'll eat out at nine.'

'But I—'

The door clipped shut and after a moment Angelique dropped her shoulders on a sigh. He had a nasty habit of getting in the last word.

She would have to break him of it.

CHAPTER EIGHT

REMY HAD BARELY stepped out of the hotel when his mobile buzzed. He looked at the screen and winced. 'Rafe, I was just about to call you and—'

'Tell me I did not just see you telling the press you've married the devil's spawn, Angelique Marchand,' Rafe said.

Remy glanced around to see if anyone was close enough to listen in. 'That's not a very nice way to speak of your brand new sister-in-law, bro.'

Rafe let out a curse. 'Are you out of your mind? What the hell are you playing at?'

'Hey, it's not Angelique's fault her old man is a double-crossing tool.' Remy couldn't help thinking how ironic it was to find himself defending her when normally he was finding any excuse to criticise her.

'Don't tell me you're in love with her, because I don't believe it for a second. The only person you love is yourself.'

'That's a bit harsh. I love lots of people. Even you.'

'Come on, Remy, this is me—Rafe. I know you. You would never fall in love with Angelique. She's as far away from your ideal woman as she could be. You've always said what a little slutty shrew she is. What's going on? Has Henri Marchand done the dirty on you? Forced you to marry her? Set up some sort of dodgy deal?'

'None of the above,' Remy said. 'Angelique followed me to Dharbiri and, to cut a long story short, she was found in my room and I had to marry her to keep from causing a public riot which might have ended up in one or both of us losing the skin off our backs. I decided not the take the chance.'

'Are you kidding me?' Rafe asked.

'Not at all,' Remy said.

'You said she followed you to Dharbiri. Why didn't you say something earlier if you were involved with her? Why let us find out like this?'

'I wasn't involved with her. Before this I hadn't seen or even spoken to her in years. She came to see me about her father's house. Remember Tarrantloch in Scotland? I won it off Henri Marchand in a bet.'

Rafe swore again but this time it was more a sound of admiration. 'So, it's just a marriage on paper, right?'

Another little silence, while Remy thought of how to answer. He didn't want to lie to his brother but neither did he want to discuss what had happened not ten minutes ago. His body was still singing from what was one of the most—if not *the* most—exciting sexual encounter of his life.

'You haven't,' Rafe said, sounding stern and incredulous at the same time.

'Hey, what *is* this?' Remy said. 'I don't ask you about your sex life with Poppy. Back off. I know what I'm doing.' *Sort of.* 'It's cool. Everything's cool.'

'You married our family's worst enemy's daughter without a pre-nup,' Rafe said. 'I don't think that's cool; I think that's outright stupidity. You're jeopardising everything we've worked for, just like *Nonno* did. Have you learned nothing in your thirty-two years on this planet?'

'What was I supposed to do?' Remy felt his hackles come up. 'Let her take the rap for being discovered in my room? I had to think, and think fast. There wasn't time to draw up a pre-nup. I did what I thought was the best and safest thing.'

'Being legally tied to Angelique Marchand is *not* safe,' Rafe said.

Tell me about it. 'I won't stay married to her for any longer than I have to,' Remy said. 'I'm working it to my advantage. Remember the Mappleton hotel chain I've been trying to buy for months? Henri Marchand's rumours about me turned old man Mappleton off, but now I'm married to Angelique he wants to play ball. I'm meeting with him next week. If I nail that deal, it will be worth any minor inconvenience of being married.'

'I can't help thinking this could blow up in your face.'

'You always think that about me,' Remy said. 'I like taking chances. Going with the gut. I always land on my feet. Always. Goal. Focus. Win. Remember?'

Rafe let out a long breath. 'Watch your back, Remy. Keeping your enemies close is wise, but sleeping with them is not.'

Sleeping with them is the fun part, Remy thought as he ended the call.

In fact, he couldn't wait to do it again.

Angelique was putting the finishing touches to her make-up when her mobile phone rang. She glanced at the screen to see it was her manager, Mackenzie Hill-strom, from her New York modelling agency. 'Hi, Mac, I was going to call you but—'

'Darling girl, I should hate you for not inviting me to your totally awesome desert wedding, and for not even telling me you were dating one of the most eligible and gorgeous men on this planet, but I forgive you, because you've just landed yourself the biggest contract of all time,' Mackenzie said.

'I...I have?'

'Forget Barbados and bikinis and bum-biting camels in Mexico. You are now the new poster girl for designer bridal wear. Every top designer wants you on his or her books! There's a bidding war going on as we speak. You looked absolutely amazing in that traditional garb. No one but you could pull that exotic look off. You've created the biggest sensation in bridal wear since the royal wedding.'

Bridal wear?

Was this fate's idea of a twisted joke? 'Um... Wow, that's great.' Should she tell her manager her marriage to Remy was only temporary, a charade unlikely to last longer than it took him to nail the Mappleton account?

'This is the big break you've been waiting for,' Mackenzie went on in her fast-paced New York accent. 'You're our golden girl now. You'll earn millions out of this. It will set you up for life—me too, when it comes to that. I'll email you the contract. Get it back to me as soon as you can. Take the next couple of weeks off while I sort the spring schedule out. Shanae will fill in for you on the Barbados shoot. Any questions?'

'No...that sounds wonderful.' *I think.*

Angelique put the phone down on the dressing table. She looked at it for a long moment, wondering if she should call her manager straight back and tell her she didn't want to take up the offer. Her life seemed to be spinning out of control in an alarming manner. A part of her wanted the money that was being put on the table, but the fame and constant exposure that would go with it gave her a troubling sense of unease. She had planned for months to get out of modelling. She was tired of living in the false world of perfection.

Her body was tired.

She had notebooks and slips of paper with designs doodled all over them. When would she have time to pursue her dream if she was caught up in a hectic shooting schedule? She didn't believe in doing things in half-measures. If they wanted her to be the next it girl in bridal wear, then her designs would have to wait…

Angelique was made up, coiffed and poised when Remy came back to the suite. She felt much more in charge when she had her professional armour on. It seemed important to give Remy the impression their love-making had made little or no impact on her. But it was hard to ignore the way her senses jumped to attention as soon as he came in the door, even harder to ignore the way her skin tightened all over and the way her inner core contracted. 'Nice walk?' she said.

His espresso gaze moved over her in a lazy sweep that tightened her skin and her inner core another notch. 'I wonder how long it would take me to get you out of that dress?'

She squared her shoulders even as her belly flipped over. 'What happened before was a mistake. I'd rather not repeat it.'

A hint of a smile lifted the corner of his mouth. 'You're not a very good liar, *ma chérie*. What happened before is going to happen again. And soon and often.'

Angelique felt a shiver course down her spine at the dark glitter of unbridled lust in his eyes. 'I think it would be foolish to complicate things with that level of involvement. We don't even like each other. It's rather unseemly to be going at each other like wild animals.'

His smile tilted a little further. 'Unseemly?'

She willed herself to hold his gaze for as long as she could. 'Primitive.'

He closed the distance between them in an easy stride or two. She knew she should have stepped back but her feet seemed to be bolted to the floor. She drew in a sharp breath when he put a hand to the nape of her neck. His warm palm was slightly rough against her soft skin and a shower of sensations spiralled through her at the delicious contact.

His eyes were so dark they looked like bottomless black pools. His mouth was so sexy, so sensually contoured, her insides shifted restlessly and her own mouth started to tingle.

'The thing is, *ma belle*, I feel very primitive when I'm around you.' His hand cupped her left cheek, his thumb pad giving one stroke over her lips that sent every nerve into a frantic dance.

Angelique's heart skipped a beat as his thighs brushed against hers. She felt the bulge of his erection. It spoke to everything that was female in her. Her senses were not sleeping or dormant now; they were wide awake and hungry for his touch. Ravenous. 'Find yourself another plaything.' She was really rather proud of how curt and cold she sounded. 'I will not be used by you.'

His thumb pad moved back over her lips, his eyes still locked on hers. 'Is that really what you want? To go back to a hands-off arrangement?'

No! 'Yes.' Angelique moistened her lips and tasted salty male. It was like tasting a powerfully addictive drug. She wanted more. Now. *Right now.*

His gaze searched hers for a pulsing moment. 'Fine.' He dropped his hand from her face and moved away.

Fine? She looked at him in numb shock. *Fine?* Why wasn't he challenging her? Why wasn't he making her eat her words? Damn it! She wanted him to make her eat her words!

He glanced at his designer watch. 'We should get going. I don't want to lose our booking; I had to pull some strings to get a table at such short notice.'

'I find that very hard to believe.' Angelique curled her lip as she picked up her purse. 'The Caffarelli name can get you a table just about anywhere, I would've thought.' *Let's see if I can push a few more of those buttons of his.* 'Maybe I'll change mine and see if I can cash in on some of the benefits.'

His expression hardened to stone. 'Don't get ahead of yourself, Angelique. This is not permanent. Don't kid yourself that it will be anything but what it is right now.'

'A war zone?' she quipped.

'Temporary.' He held the door open with a pointed look. 'Shall we?'

It was a popular restaurant owned and operated by one of Britain's celebrity chefs, which meant it was a famous-person hot spot, so the paparazzi were nearly always on hand.

Angelique quailed at the thought of fending off another round of intrusive questions. She was a pretty good actor but any body-language expert worth his or her credentials would be able to see Remy was still angry with her. He hadn't spoken a word to her during the short trip to the restaurant. He had spent the entire time tapping emails into his phone.

'Couldn't we have stayed and dined in the hotel?' she asked as he helped her from the limousine.

'No.' His hand was firm as it took hers.

'But surely we should be avoiding all this attention as much as possible?' She gave him a pouty glance. 'Anyway, what will people think? We're supposed to be on our honeymoon. Eating's supposed to be the last thing on our minds.'

'Yes, well, it's probably the last thing on *your* mind, but I'm starving. I need food and I need it now.'

Angelique rolled one shoulder haughtily. 'Why are men at the mercy of their basest desires?'

He gave her a glinting look. 'Why do women deny their needs as if it's something to be ashamed of? It's not wrong to feel hungry or horny. It's completely natural.'

'You know something?' She frowned at him. 'I've always really hated that word.'

'What, hungry?'

'Horny. It's sounds…I don't know. Coarse.'

A mocking smile angled his mouth. 'So underneath that brash, streetwise exterior is a sweet old-fashioned girl? Don't make me laugh.'

Angelique glared at him. 'You don't know me. Not the real me.' *No one knows the real me.*

He tucked her arm through one of his as he led her into the restaurant. 'Maybe now's a good time to start.'

Dining out for Angelique was like sharing a room with Remy—full of wicked temptation. Being tired and emotionally out of sorts made it much harder for her to rely on her steely resolve to keep to her strict diet. Just like kissing or touching Remy, one taste was enough to throw caution to the wind. Making love with him had changed everything. It was like trying to eat one peanut or one French fry: it was impossible; she would always want more. More of him. *All* of him. But how could she have him when he didn't want this arrangement to last any longer than it took to seal his latest business coup?

The Caffarelli brothers—before Rafe had married and Raoul had become engaged—had written the rule-book for rakes. Of the three of them, Remy had the worst reputation for the rate of turnover of partners. He had never had a relationship last more than a week or two.

But then, why would he?

He was spoilt for choice. Women adored him and flocked about him like bees around blossom. He was never in one place longer than a week at a time, which of course made it easy for him to be casual about his hook-ups.

Did he ever want more than just sex? Did he ever think about the companionship and loyalty his brothers were now experiencing? Did he think about the promise of stability and a love that would last through good times and bad? To have someone to share the bond of children with, to watch as they grew from babies to children to adulthood? To love and protect them, nurture them and teach them how to be good, trustworthy citizens?

Angelique's brow furrowed as she looked down at the menu. Instead of the words printed there, she started to picture a tiny baby with a shock of jet-black hair and big brown eyes fringed with dark lashes.

Remy said he didn't want children.

She had said the same. Many times.

But it wasn't quite true...

'By the way.' Remy looked up from the menu he was perusing. 'We are not leaving this restaurant until I've seen you eat something. Understood?'

Angelique's back prickled. 'I have to think of my figure, especially now.'

'Why especially now?'

She gave him an imperious look. 'You're not the only one getting a ratings boost from our marriage.'

He cocked his head in interest. 'Oh, really?'

'My manager is firming up a new contract for me to consider. Once I sign it, I'm going to be booked up for months and months.'

'Tell them to wait. Tell them you're not available until after Christmas. I want you with me for the next month or two at the very least.'

Angelique felt her heart give a little skip at the thought of him wanting her with him but then she remembered his precious business deal. He wanted her for show, not for her.

It was an act.

A game of charades.

Even though technically she was free to be with him while her manager negotiated the schedule, she resented him arrogantly assuming she would drop everything just because he told her to.

She was *not* going to be ordered about by him.

'Do you really think you can just march into my life and take control as if I have no mind or will of my own?'

He gave her a knowing look. 'I didn't come marching into your life. You came blundering into mine. Now it's time for you to take responsibility for it.'

'By following you around like a stupid little lapdog?' She gave an exaggerated shudder of distaste before curling her lip at him. 'I don't think so.'

His mouth flattened and his eyes flashed her a warning. 'You will do as I say or I'll take everything off your father. Do you hear me? Everything. There won't be a penny left for you to inherit once I'm done with him. Don't say I didn't warn you.'

Angelique pressed her spine back against the supports of her chair. 'Do you really think I will respond to threats?'

'You will if you know what's good for you.'

What would be good for me would be to put as much distance between you and me as is globally possible.

It was too dangerous being with him. How soon before she caved in and fell into his arms again? She had to get away. She had to think. Clear her head.

Protect her heart.

Angelique put her napkin down on the table and pushed back her chair. 'Will you excuse me?'

His brows snapped together. 'Where are you going?'

'I'm going to the powder room.' She gave him a lofty look. She didn't have to tell him *which* powder room. *Like one several thousand kilometres away.* 'Do I need to ask your permission first?'

His dark, unreadable eyes measured hers for a moment. 'Fine. Go and powder your nose. But if you're not back here in two minutes I'll come and find you.'

I'll be miles away by then.

Angelique only got as far as the street when she was stopped, not by Remy but by her father. He came striding towards her from the cab he had just vacated. His cheeks were puce and his brows were joined over his formidable nose.

'Is it true?' he asked. 'Have you married Remy Caffarelli?'

It was probably perverse of her, but she felt a strange sense of satisfaction at having done something so shocking and outrageously disappointing to her father. He looked like he was having a conniption. 'News certainly travels fast in this city,' she said lightly. 'How did you find out?'

He gave her a poisonous glare. 'Do you have any idea of the utter fool you've made of me? I was at my club when one of my colleagues informed me. He read a tweet about it. There was a photo of you in a wedding outfit that looked like something out of *The Arabian Nights*. How could you do this to me? You couldn't have thought of a worse punishment, you silly little cow. Have you no brain in that stupid, big, fat ugly head of yours?'

'Apologise to my wife or I'll flatten you.'

Angelique spun around to see Remy standing there. He had a grim look on his face and his fists were clenching as if he was already rehearsing his first punch. 'Don't.' She put her hand on his arm. 'It's not worth it.'

He gently but firmly unpeeled her fingers from his wrist and faced her father. He spoke in French and it wasn't pretty. Angelique watched as her father's face went from puce to bright crimson and then back to puce. Even the tips of his ears were bright red, as if he was going to explode on the spot.

'She is my daughter,' Henri said through tight lips. 'I'll speak to her any way I like.'

Remy suddenly seemed so incredibly tall as he stared down her father. 'She is my wife and no one gets to speak to her like that.' His tone was commanding, authoritative. Intractable. 'Apologise now or suffer the consequences.'

Her father huffed and puffed but finally he muttered what one could only very loosely describe as an apology before he sloped off back into his cab like a chastened dog being sent to its kennel.

Remy put a protective arm around Angelique's waist. 'Does he normally speak to you like that?'

She pressed her lips together as she watched the lights of the cab fade into the distance. She felt a sudden desire to cry and had to blink a few times to get control. No one had ever come to her defence before. Her mother had been too weak; the household staff too scared of losing their jobs.

'*Ma petite?*'

Angelique looked up at him. Had he ever looked more handsome, more dashing and gorgeous than right now? How could she ever have thought she hated him? She quickly shielded her gaze. 'We don't have the best relationship. His short fuse and my smart mouth aren't a good combination for familial harmony.'

He brushed her cheek with a light-as-air glide of his finger. 'Has he ever laid a hand on you?'

'No. But he uses words just as lethally. He did it to my mother. I'm sure it caused her breakdown. She just couldn't take it any more.'

His expression flashed with disgust. 'Why didn't you say something earlier? I would have sorted him out years ago.'

Angelique gave a weary sigh. 'I wanted to plenty of times but who would've believed me? It would blot his copybook too much to be seen as anything but a devoted father. The fact that he bawled me out like that in such a public place is a testament to how much he hates you. He would normally never speak to me like that if there was an audience.'

Remy took her hands and gave them a light squeeze. 'Promise me something.'

'What?'

'Don't ever be alone with him. Ever. Do you understand? Never.'

Right at this very moment, Angelique would have promised him anything. 'I promise.'

'Good girl.' He brought her hands up to his mouth and kissed both of them in turn, his eyes still holding hers. 'So, tell me about this new contract. You didn't get round to telling what it was about.'

She gave her eyes a little roll. 'You're not going to believe what they want me to do.'

His brows snapped together. 'Not a naked shoot?'

Angelique laughed at his fierce expression. 'No, nothing like that. I'm to be the new poster girl for designer bridal wear.'

'Bridal wear?'

'Yes. How ironic is that? I never even wanted to be a bride and now I'm going to be wearing frothy wedding dresses and voluminous veils every day of the week, and earning millions for the privilege.'

His dark gaze searched hers for a moment. 'And you're pleased?'

Angelique pasted on her brightest smile. 'But of course. For one thing, I won't have to diet so stringently. Just think of the multitude of sins I can hide under a hoop skirt.'

A smile kicked up the corners of his mouth. 'This calls for a celebration. Want to go back to the hotel and order in room service?'

'But what about the table you had to work so hard to secure?'

He gave a shrug. 'Personally, I think the place is overrated. My brother Rafe's wife, Poppy, would probably agree with me. Did I tell you she's a cook?'

'I think I read that somewhere.' She fell into step

beside him as they walked along the footpath. 'What's she like?'

'Gorgeous.' He gave her a sudden grin. 'I mean that in a brother-in-law kind of way, of course. She reminds me of my mother. So does Raoul's fiancée, Lily. They're both really lovely girls. A bit too homespun for me, but still, each to his own.'

'Careful, Remy, you're starting to sound envious.'

He shook his head, his smile fading away. 'I'm not cut out for that domestic scene. I'm like you; I like my freedom too much. Babies seem such smelly, noisy things. And then they grow up and become annoying smart-mouthed tearaways who keep their parents up all night worrying about them. No. Not for me. Definitely not.'

Angelique gave him a playful little shoulder-bump. 'I'm sure not all children turn out horribly spoilt, obnoxious brats like you and me.'

He gave her a crooked grin as he gently shoulder-bumped her back. 'God forbid.'

CHAPTER NINE

REMY WATCHED an hour later in their suite as Angelique nibbled at an undressed green salad and took occasional sips from a glass of Chianti. When she wasn't acting tough and being lippy, she was surprisingly good company. Quirky. Funny. Engaging.

Something had shifted in their relationship outside the restaurant.

He had been brought up to defend and protect women. Not by his grandfather, who exploited them any chance he could, but by his father before he had died and his two older brothers. Remy didn't mind the occasional verbal brawl, but insulting a woman and calling her names was not something he could ever tolerate.

He had never liked Angelique's father, even when Henri had been a regular visitor at his grandfather's villa in Rome, well before he had come across him in business. Remy had always found him two-faced, sly and conniving. The fact that Henri had been verbally abusing his wife and daughter disgusted Remy but it didn't surprise him. Men like Henri Marchand used power in dishonourable ways. They snatched at it whenever they could and gave little thought to the harm they were causing others.

Remy wondered if Angelique's wilful and at times

reckless behaviour was a reaction to the tyranny she had lived under for so long. While she didn't live with her father, and hadn't for a long time, he still seemed to have power to hurt her. He'd seen the way she'd flinched at Henri's horrible words. It was no wonder she was so adamantly opposed to marriage since the example set for her had been so appalling.

Protecting her had been an automatic reaction for Remy. He had been prepared to use force if he'd had to, although generally he didn't condone physical violence. His anger at her escaping from the restaurant had turned so quickly into something else.

He still wasn't quite sure exactly what it was…

'Do you want some more wine?'

Angelique shook her head. 'No, one is enough. I'm not a big drinker. Too many calories.'

Remy frowned as he looked at her barely touched meal. 'This new contract… How does that fit in with your plans to focus on designing?'

She put her glass back down and met his gaze. 'It'll take ages, possibly months or even up to a year, to get to the manufacturing and selling stage. I'll need an income in the meantime. I can't live on air.'

He gave her a dry look. 'You're doing a pretty fine job of it so far. You've only taken a couple of nibbles of that piece of lettuce.'

'I don't need a lot of food.' She gave his empty plate a baleful glance. 'Unlike some people, who have disgustingly voracious appetites and seemingly hollow legs.'

'I'm not a glutton. I just love food.'

She arched a neatly groomed eyebrow in a worldly manner. 'And sex.'

He gave her a glinting smile. 'That too.'

There was a little silence.

She passed the tip of her tongue over her lush lips and an arrow of lust speared Remy in the groin. Was she thinking of their passionate union earlier?

He hadn't *stopped* thinking about it.

He hadn't stopped feeling it tingling in his flesh like aftershocks in the wake of earthquake. He could still taste her sweet vanilla and milk taste. He could still feel the softness of her lips, the boldness of her clever little tongue, the smooth glide of her hands and fingers.

He suppressed a shudder as he thought of what that mouth and those hands could do to him. What that gorgeously tight, feminine body *had* done to him.

Made him lose control.

'We're going to have to share that bed,' Remy said. 'Maybe we should put down some ground rules first.'

'What do you suggest?' Her expression was pert. 'A chalk line down the middle?'

'I was thinking more of a roll of pillows or a bolster.'

'How about a barbed wire fence?'

Remy felt another arrow hit bull's-eye. 'I wouldn't want you to get hurt when you head over to my side.'

She gave him an arch look. 'What makes you think I would come over to your side?'

'You think we can keep this thing between us on ice? Seriously, how long do you think that's going to last? You're hot for me. You can deny it all you like, but I know you want me. You've always wanted me.' *Like I've always wanted you.*

She flickered her eyes upwards. 'I can't believe the size of your ego. I might have wanted you, but I've *had* you, and quite frankly once is more than enough.'

Remy felt the rush of a fresh challenge fire through his blood. She was playing hard to get. It was another point-scoring game to her. She had sensed his weakness and was going in for the kill.

Did she want him to beg?

He would *never* do that.

He could live without sex—for a while. Sure he could. Monks did it all the time. It was supposed to be good for the mind. It was supposed to be mentally cleansing…or something.

'So, what are you saying? I didn't float your boat or something?'

'The sails gave a little flutter but that was about it.'

She was lying. He had felt her spasms and he had heard her cries. Unless she was a very good actress, she'd had the orgasm of her life. Why then was she so keen not to repeat it? 'If you change your mind then just lean over and tap me on the shoulder,' he said. 'I'll be happy to get your motor started.'

She gave him a withering look. 'Don't hold your breath.'

Angelique came out of the bathroom half an hour later to find Remy lying on his back with an e-reader flopped down on his chest. His eyes were closed, his breathing was steady and even, his body naked from the waist up. She wasn't sure if he was naked below the waist, because the sheet was covering him, but she had a feeling he wasn't the type of guy to wear pyjamas to bed.

She let her eyes feast on his naked chest and broad shoulders. Each muscle was so perfectly contoured, toned and taut with not an ounce of excess flesh on him anywhere. His hair was tousled, as if he had not long ago run his fingers through it, and his face was shadowed with evening stubble.

All of the Caffarelli brothers were staggeringly gor-

geous but Angelique had always found Remy's dark
features particularly so. It was something about his
chocolate-brown eyes, the way they glinted with amusement or mockery even when he was doing his deadpan
thing. It was the way his mouth was fashioned, the lower
lip fuller than the top one. The chiselled leanness of his
jaw; the way he always looked like he hadn't shaved
closely enough. It was something about his hands with
their long, tanned fingers that felt like a Taser zap when
they touched her.

Angelique carefully approached his side of the bed
and lifted the e-reader off his chest. He made a low mur-
mur and she paused before she put the e-reader on the
bedside table. She tiptoed round to her side of the bed,
gently peeled back the covers, slipped in and huddled
right on the edge so no part of her body was anywhere
near his. She closed her eyes and willed herself to sleep
but the citrus scent of his aftershave stirred her senses.
She could feel the warmth of his body; it seemed to
be reaching out to her, enveloping her...*tempting her.*

She jammed her eyes even tighter together and
brought the covers right up to her chin.

She would not touch him!

Angelique must have drifted off eventually because
she when she opened her eyes it was light and Remy
was already up, showered and dressed. He'd dropped
the towel he'd used over the back of the velvet covered
chair he was now sitting on as he typed something into
his phone, a heavy frown between his brows.

'Don't you *ever* pick up after yourself?'

'Hmm?' His tone was absent and he didn't even look
her way as he kept typing.

Angelique swung her legs over the side of the bed,

slipped her arms through her wrap and tied it around her body. She came over to where he was sitting, picked up the damp towel and held it between two fingers. 'Do you ever spare a thought for the person who has to come in and service your room?'

'What?' He glanced at her then, his expression still dark with a frown.

'You leave stuff everywhere. The least you could do is hang your towel up or leave it in the tub or the shower cubicle if you're not going to use it again.' She put her hands on her hips and glowered at him. 'Stop typing when I'm talking to you!'

'You're not talking to me, you're nagging me.'

'Yes, well, that's what wives are forced to do, because their lazy husbands don't see the hours of invisible work that goes on behind the scenes to keep a house running smoothly.'

He rose to his feet and Angelique took a little step back. Without her heels he towered over her and she had to crick her neck to keep eye contact. His expression was mocking as he looked down at her. 'And just how many houses have you run, *ma chérie*?'

She pursed her lips. 'I'm just saying…'

He held her gaze for a long moment. He seemed to be thinking about something. She could see his mouth shifting from side to side in a contemplative manner. 'Can you cook?'

'Yes. I've been to cookery schools in France, Italy and Thailand. Why?'

'Would you cook a dinner for me?'

Angelique frowned. 'What, you mean every day, like in a traditional marriage?'

'No, nothing like that. I want to entertain Robert Mappleton—you know, the guy I've been trying to win over? He's ultra-conservative and traditional. He's been wined and dined thousands of times in the best restaurants across the globe. What I think would really impress him is a home-cooked dinner in a private setting. Will you do it?'

She caught her lower lip between her teeth. The sooner she helped Remy nail his deal, the sooner they could go their separate ways. That certainly wasn't half as attractive as it had been a day or so ago. She had her own contract to consider now. Would the top-end designers currently courting her still want her if she was divorced?

Probably not.

'Which private setting did you have in mind?'

'Tarrantloch.'

Angelique glared at him. 'You insensitive bastard!'

'What?'

She narrowed her gaze to slits. 'You really are the most unfeeling jerk I've ever come across. How much more do you want to rub my nose in it? You stole my house and now you want me to play the 1950s housewife in it? Arrggh!'

'I guess that's a no?'

Angelique glowered at him. 'You're damn right it's a no. How could you be so cruel?'

'I was actually thinking of you,' he said. 'I thought you'd be more comfortable cooking in a familiar kitchen.'

'I'd be more comfortable if the deeds to my home were back in my hands where they belong.'

He gave her a dry look. 'Then perhaps you need to work on charming me into changing my mind, *ma petite*, hmm?'

Angelique felt a traitorous spurt of longing assail her.

How did he do that to her with just one look? Those dark eyes smouldered and she was instantly aflame. How was she going to resist him when all she wanted was to be back in his arms?

But she wasn't going to let him know that.

She narrowed her eyes even further. 'Are you blackmailing me?'

'I prefer to call it negotiating.'

'Negotiating my foot! You want me to sleep with you. Why don't you come right out and say it?'

His eyes scorched hers. 'I want to sleep with you.'

Angelique's inner core contracted. Her breasts tingled. Her heart skipped and then raced. She ran her tongue over her suddenly dry mouth. She saw the raw, naked lust in his dark eyes. She felt it in the crackling air she was trying to drag into her lungs. She felt it in the firm grip of his steely hands as they captured her by the hips and pulled her against him.

Heat against heat.

His mouth came down, hovering just above hers. 'This is what I want.' He toyed with her lips in a tantalising little tug-and-release game that made her spine turn to liquid.

I want it too. So, so much!

'And this…' He stroked the seam of her mouth with his tongue, teasing the sensitive flesh, taking possession as soon as she opened to him.

She tried to smother a whimper but her bones were melting like an ice sculpture in the Dharbiri desert sun as he explored every corner in intimate detail. One of his hands went to the small of her back, pushing her closer to his hot, hard heat, the other deftly untying the ties of her wrap and unpeeling it from her body.

He pushed aside the satin straps of her nightgown

and it slipped off her body and pooled at her feet. His hand cupped her breast, her nipple brushing against his palm, making her senses hum with delight. Need unfurled in her body, stretching like a sun-warmed cat, reaching into all of her limbs, making them soft and pliant as he crushed her to him.

Angelique tugged his shirt out of his trousers and blindly undid the buttons as her mouth fed off his. She unhitched his belt, undid his waistband, rolled down his zipper and then boldly took possession of him. He groaned into her mouth as he kicked off his shoes and stepped out of his trousers.

They stumbled back towards the bed, knocking one of the table lamps over in the process. He came down over her, his thighs trapping hers, his mouth still working its heady magic on hers.

Angelique arched her back as he left her mouth to concentrate on her breasts. The feel of his tongue and teeth on her flesh was a blissful torture. She writhed and gasped and clutched at his head.

He didn't stop at her breasts. He went lower to the cave of her belly button, dipping in and out with his moist tongue, laving her flesh, trailing even lower.

She automatically tensed. This was so personal. So very intimate.

He calmed her with a gentle hand on her thigh. 'Not comfortable with this?'

Angelique felt a blush crawl into her cheeks. He thought she was so hip and worldly but this was the one thing she had never felt comfortable sharing with any partner. It was all very well, pretending to have an orgasm when someone was rocking and humping above her, but *this* was something else. 'Um…'

'It's fine, *ma petite*. You don't have to do anything you're not comfortable with.'

Was it the fact he had given her the freedom to say no that made her now want to say yes? She slowly met his dark gaze. 'I've never done this with a partner…'

Something moved in his eyes. A flicker of surprise? Delight? 'Do you trust me to make it good for you?'

Angelique suddenly realised she did. Hadn't he already shown her what her body was capable of in terms of pleasure? She had never experienced anything like the supremely passionate response she had felt in his arms with anyone else. She wanted to experience *this* with him; this incredible intimacy would leave her with something precious and unique to remember when their marriage was over. 'Yes…'

He gently caressed her thighs, waiting until she was open and relaxed before he traced her folds with his tongue. All of her nerves writhed and danced, twirled and fretted for more. He did it again, separating her this time, tasting her, briefly touching her clitoris to give it time to get accustomed to the sensation. He slowly built the movements of his tongue against her swollen flesh, making her shiver all over as tiny ripples began to course through her. He was patient and gentle. Experimental. Gauging her response, learning her body's secrets and indulging her senses until she was suspended on a precipice, hovering, wanting, aching, but not quite able to take that final plunge.

'Come for me, *ma petite*,' he coaxed her softly. 'Don't hold back.'

'I want to but I can't.'

'Yes you can.' He stroked her tensed up thighs until they released. 'You can do it. Just stop thinking and let go.'

Angelique felt the flickering of his tongue against her and a wave of pleasure came rolling up from deep inside her. She felt every muscle in her body tighten before the final lift off. She went careening into oblivion, shuddering and shaking as the tide of release passed through her like a powerful relaxant.

Remy came back over her and pushed her wild hair back off her face. 'Average?'

Angelique couldn't stop a coy smile. 'How do I know, since I don't have anything to compare it to?'

His gave her one of his smouldering looks. 'I can soon fix that.'

'Wait.' She put a hand on his chest, her gaze sultry. 'There's something I have to see to first.'

He drew in an audible breath as her hand moved down his body. But she wasn't content with just stroking and caressing him. She wanted to taste him as he had tasted her. This was another act she had shied away from in the past, but right now it seemed perfectly natural to pleasure him with her lips and tongue.

She pressed a pathway of kisses down his chest, swirling her tongue into his belly button before going inexorably lower. She felt his abdominal muscles contract the closer she got to her target. She breathed over his erection at first, letting him feel the dance of her breath, letting him experience the anticipation of her imminent possession.

'I usually put a condom on at this point.' His voice sounded rough. Gravelly.

Angelique gave him a seductive look from beneath her lashes. 'There isn't time.'

'But I— *Oh God*.' He sucked in another breath as she set to work on him.

It was thrilling to have him so in her power. She

had never realised how arousing it was to feel him and hear him struggle for control. She was ruthless as she drew on him, not giving him a chance to pull away. She tasted the hot essence of him against her tongue, felt the tension in him against her lips as she moved them up and down his shaft.

He grabbed at her head with both of his hands, presumably to push her away, but she refused to budge. She hummed against his swollen flesh and he gave a quickly muttered curse and then spilled.

After it was over he fell on the bed on his back, his chest rising and falling as he tried to get his breathing under control.

Angelique trailed a light fingertip up and down his chest. 'Better than average?'

He turned his head and gave her a sinfully erotic look. 'The best.'

'Are you just saying that?'

'No.'

Wow. Oh wow. Her fingertip came back up and circled one of his flat, dark nipples. 'How soon before you can go again?'

'Why do you ask?'

She gave a casual little shrug. 'Just wondering.'

He rolled her back over and trapped her within the cage of his arms. 'You still want to play, *mon trésor*?'

She traced his lower lip with her fingertip. 'Might as well make the most of our time together.'

He stopped the pathway of her finger by holding her hand in his. 'Just so we're clear on this—I'm not making any promises about Tarrantloch. I won it fair and square. I don't do sentimentality or guilt trips. You need to understand and accept that.'

'But I thought you said—'

'If we continue to sleep together, it's because we want to satisfy the mutual attraction we feel. It's not about and should not be about anything else.'

Angelique knew how determined he could be, but then so could she. Clearly locking horns with him wasn't going to work. It had never worked before. She would be better served in finding another way to appeal to his sense of fairness—assuming he had one, of course. Charm him. Woo him. Beguile him. *Outsmart him.*

She tiptoed a fingertip down his sternum again. 'Do you ever *not* get your way?'

He gave her a lazy smile. 'Giving in is about as much in my nature as submission and demureness is in yours.'

'I don't know about that.' Angelique gave a little sinuous movement beneath him. 'I'm feeling pretty submissive right now.'

His eyes glinted as his hands pinned her arms either side of her head, his strong thighs trapping hers with erotic intent. 'Then I'd better make the most of it.'

And he did.

CHAPTER TEN

ANGELIQUE BREATHED IN the sharp, clean air of the highlands as Remy helped her out of the car the following day. Tarrantloch in autumn was bleak and cold but that was part of the raw beauty of it. The turreted grey stone mansion had been in her mother's family for over three-hundred years. It was set in a large verdant clearing in the middle of a forest and had its own lake and a burn that ran with ice-cold water full of salmon and trout.

She had spent some of her happiest times here as a child before her mother had turned into a browbeaten shadow of her former self. Coming here had been something Angelique and her mother had done together in the early days to spend time with her maternal grandparents while Henri had been busy with his business affairs in Europe.

But, once her grandparents had passed away within a year of each other, Tarrantloch had been left idle with just a handful of servants, as her father had insisted on living in his homeland of France so he could commute more easily to Italy, where he had his major business interests, including those with Vittorio Caffarelli.

Over the last couple of years, however, he had come back and taken up residence, strutting around like a proud peacock as he conducted various house parties with his business cronies. It disgusted Angelique to see her mother's home exploited by her father and she had mostly kept well away unless she knew he was abroad on business.

Angelique hadn't been to Tarrantloch since the summer when she'd had a ten-day break from her schedule. It seemed surreal to be here now, officially married to Remy, knowing the house was no longer hers.

Might never be hers again.

Remy had decided he wanted it as a trophy. What else could it be to him other than a prize to gloat over? He had luxury homes all over Europe and the Mediterranean. Besides, if he wanted to see snow he could go to his chalet in the Swiss Alps.

No, Tarrantloch was his way of publicly claiming victory over her father. What pained her the most was Remy could so easily turn around and sell it once it had served its purpose. And, one thing she knew for certain, he wouldn't be offering it to her for mate's rates. He was a ruthless, hard-nosed businessman. He wouldn't allow sentimentality or emotions to influence him.

But she was not going to give up until she had exhausted every possible avenue to get it back.

Angelique walked with Remy over the pebbled driveway to the front door. 'Have you kept on any of my father's staff?' she asked.

'None, apart from the gardener, and he's on notice.'

She raised a brow. 'Why not?'

'Because not one of them was doing a proper day's work.' He took out the keys he had in his pocket and unlocked the heavy door. 'I'm going to conduct some interviews while we're here. I want to employ locals, people who know the house and want it to be preserved. Your

father surrounded himself with a motley crew of syco-
phants who didn't do much more than take up space.'

Angelique was inclined to agree with him. More than
inclined. She had never liked the obsequious butler and
housekeeper her father had hired. The devoted staff her
grandparents had employed had left in dribs and drabs
over the years, either through retirement, death or dis-
enchantment. 'So who's here now?'

'Just us.'

She blinked. 'What? No one at all? Just us?' *Alone?*

He gave her a wickedly sexy smile. 'It's our honeymoon, *ma chérie*. We're not supposed to have people
with us.'

Her belly gave a little quivery swoop. 'But what
about the dinner with Robert Mappleton? After all,
isn't that why we're here?'

'That's not until the end of next week.'

'Why not get it over with this week?'

'Ah, but that would appear too eager, *n'est-ce pas*?
Better to let him think I'm in no great hurry to play
ball.'

Angelique sent him a wry look. 'I can see why you've
accumulated the wealth you have at such a young age:
you're as cunning as a fox.'

He grinned as he held the door open for her. 'No
point in being too predictable. Where's the fun in that?
No, my philosophy is to keep them guessing for as long
as you can and then reel them in when they least expect it.'

Is that what you're doing with me? Angelique wondered as she followed him inside. Hadn't she already
been reeled in? She had been so determined to keep
out of his bed, to keep immune to his potent charm, but
as soon as he'd kissed her at the wedding ceremony in

Dharbiri her fate had been sealed. What hope did she have resisting him when his passionate possession made her feel so alive and vital as a woman?

Coming here with him for a two-week 'honeymoon' was only going to make her need of him all the more entrenched. She knew that, but had come anyway, even though she could have made up some excuse to do with her new contract. She had signed and emailed it earlier that day. Her manager had already lined up a shoot with three of the biggest names in haute couture in Paris.

Angelique rubbed her hands up and down her arms as the chilly air of the old house goose-bumped her skin. 'Right now I'm kind of wishing I had gone to Barbados.'

Remy flashed her a quick grin. 'Where's your sense of adventure, *ma petite*? It won't take long to lay a fire.'

'There's central heating. The main switch is over there.'

'I'll see to it and the luggage while you have a wander around. Make yourself at home.'

She gave him a flinty look. 'Excuse me, but up until a few days ago this *was* my home.'

'Then you won't need me to take you on a guided tour, will you?'

Angelique glowered at him. 'Why are you doing this? Why are you rubbing my nose in it like this? I realise you have issues with my father over what happened between him and your grandfather but that's nothing to do with me. I didn't do any dodgy deals. Why am I the scapegoat?'

His look was brooding and intractable. 'This isn't about you, Angelique. Last year your father circulated rumours about me that cost me millions. I don't take that sort of stuff lying down. I wanted revenge, not just for myself but also for what happened to my family. My grandfather almost lost everything when your father pulled the rug from under him.'

'You don't even like your grandfather!' Angelique threw back. 'Why are you so keen to get justice for him?'

'I'm not getting it for him,' Remy said. 'I'm getting it for Rafe. He worked harder than any of us to rebuild our assets. Rafe has always shouldered the responsibility of looking after Raoul and me. I wanted to do my bit to show him his sacrifice hadn't gone unnoticed or been taken for granted.'

'Don't you care that you're hurting me in the process?'

'How am I hurting you?' His expression turned mocking. 'You're the one who just landed a multimillion-dollar contract simply because you're married to me. I have yet to reap any benefits, especially if this Mappleton deal falls through.'

But I don't even want that contract. I shouldn't have signed it. I wish I hadn't.

Angelique pushed the errant thoughts back and planted her hands on her hips. 'I seem to recollect you got some fringe benefits last night.'

His eyes started to smoulder as he closed the distance between them in a couple of lazy strides. 'I didn't hear you complaining.'

She pushed her bottom lip out in a pout. 'I have bruises.'

A frown flickered across his forehead. 'Where?'

Angelique turned over her wrists to show him where his fingers had faintly marked her skin when he'd held her down the night before. Every time she saw the tiny marks she felt a shudder of remembered pleasure go through her. It had been like being branded by him.

Owned by him. Controlled by him. She had been more than willing, which somehow made it worse. She didn't want to need him in such an intensely physical way. She had always been the one in control with men in the past. Being dominated by Remy, even playfully during sex, made her feel as if she was relinquishing all power to him, especially when he still hadn't told her if he was going to give her back her home.

He took her left wrist, brought it up to his mouth and gently brushed his lips against the almost imperceptible mark. 'I'm sorry. I didn't realise I'd hurt you.'

She felt a traitorous ribbon of desire unfurl inside her. 'You didn't hurt me. I just have a tendency to bruise easily.'

His thumb moved over her pulse point. 'Maybe you should be the one who does the tying up next time.'

Angelique arched a brow. 'You'd let me do that?'

His eyes smouldered some more. 'Only if I knew I could get out of it.'

Like our marriage.

It wasn't for ever. He wanted to be free as soon as his business deal was signed and secured. The bitter irony was *she* was going to help him achieve it. She would be breaking her own heart. Trashing her dreams. Ruining her hopes.

There would be no happy-ever-after with Remy.

It was foolish to dream of black-haired babies with chocolate-brown eyes. It was crazy to think Remy would ever utter an endearment he actually meant. It was madness to want him to fall in love with her.

It was madness to have fallen in love with him.

She would have to fall out of love with him. Quick smart. It would be the ultimate in humiliation to have him find out how she felt. It sounded so pathetic, being hopelessly in love with someone since you were sixteen.

Unrequited love.

Obsessive love.

That was all it was—a fantasy. A teenage infatuation that had grown into an adult fixation.

The sooner she got over it the better.

Angelique stepped back from him with a casual air. 'What plans have you made about food and so on? I'm pretty sure my father wouldn't have left anything healthy and nutritious in the pantry.'

'I've organised a food parcel from our hotel in London. It's in the car with our luggage. I'll do some more shopping tomorrow.'

She widened her eyes in mock surprise. 'You actually *know* how to shop for food?'

'I do occasionally pick up the odd item or two. I quite enjoy it.' He turned to the thermostat on the wall and began adjusting the temperature settings. 'My mother used to take us shopping with her. She was keen for us to experience as normal a life as possible because she hadn't been born to money or privilege. If we behaved well, she'd buy us a *gelato* at the end.' His hand dropped from the panel and he turned. He had a wistful expression on his face. 'Rafe would always have chocolate, Raoul would always have lemon, but I used to have a different flavour each time…'

Angelique studied him for a moment. He looked like he was mentally recalling each and every one of those outings with his mother. The boating accident on the French Riviera that had killed his parents had occurred the year before she had been born. She had only ever known the Caffarelli brothers as orphans. From her youthful perspective they had always seemed terribly sophisticated and racy, with their eye-popping good looks and wealthy lifestyle. But behind the trappings of wealth and privilege was a tragedy that had robbed three little boys of their loving parents.

Angelique remembered too well the shock of feeling alone. The utter desperation she had felt at seeing her mother's body lowered into the ground on the dismally wet and grey morning of the funeral was something she would never forget. The build-up of emotion inside her chest had felt like a tsunami about to break. But somehow she had kept it in because she hadn't wanted to disappoint her father. He had said she must be brave and so she was. But inside a part of her had died and gone with her mother into that cold, black hole in the ground.

Angelique blinked away the memory and said, 'It must have been devastating for you when your parents were killed.'

A screen came down over his face. 'I got over it.' He moved past her to go back outside to get their bags. 'Stay inside out of the cold. I won't be long.'

Had he really got over it? He had only been seven years old. It was young for any child to lose a parent, yet he had not lost one but both. Angelique suspected that, like her, his restlessness and wild, partying lifestyle had come out of that deep pain of being abandoned so suddenly and so young. He was anchorless and yet shied away from anything that would tie him down.

His grandfather Vittorio could not be described as a nurturer. He was a cold, hard, bitter man with a tendency to lose his temper at the least provocation. She hadn't seen Vittorio for a number of years, but in the old days when she and her father had been regular visitors to the Caffarelli villa in Rome she had given him a wide berth.

Of the three boys Remy seemed the most willing to deal with his grandfather. He visited him more often than his brothers and seemed to have a better relationship with him than either Rafe or Raoul, possibly because Remy had always relied on his natural charm to win people over.

Angelique wondered if Vittorio had found out about their marriage yet. It had been three days and as far as she knew Remy hadn't called or spoken to him other than what he'd said on camera when the press had stormed them.

What did his brothers think? Had they contacted him and told him what a fool he was for marrying someone like her? She had always been a bit frightened of Rafe, who was so much older, but Raoul had always been nice to her.

Would he too think it was the worst disaster in the world for Remy to be locked in a marriage with her?

Remy was dusting the snow off his shoulders as he came inside when his phone rang. He knew it was his grandfather because he had set a particular ringtone to Vittorio's number. He deliberately hadn't called Vittorio before now to talk about his marriage to Angelique because that was what his grandfather would have expected, and Remy had learned over time that it was more tactical to do what he *didn't* expect. It gave him more leverage with the old man and, he liked to think, a measure of respect. '*Nonno*, nice of you to call. What's new?'

'I have a newspaper in front of me that says you've married Angelique Marchand.' His grandfather's voice had that thread of steel in it that used to terrify Remy as a young child. 'There's also a photo of you together outside some hotel in London.'

'Is it a nice photo?' Remy asked. 'She'll be hell to live with if it isn't.'

He heard Vittorio's intake of breath. 'Is this a set-up? One of your pranks to gain publicity or something?'

'It's no prank. We're married and we're staying married.' *Until I have that Mappleton deal in the bag.* Not that he could tell his grandfather that. If old man Mappleton got a hint that Remy's marriage to Angelique wasn't authentic, he would pull the plug on any negotiations.

'You always did have a thing for that girl,' Vittorio said.

Remy hadn't realised he'd been so transparent about lusting over her in the past. He'd thought he'd done a pretty good job of disguising it. 'Yes, well, you've seen what she looks like. I'm only human.'

'Why didn't you just screw her and get her out of your system?' Vittorio continued. 'Why on earth did you marry her? Have you got her pregnant or something?'

Remy gave himself a mental shake when an image of Angelique with a baby bump came to mind. 'No, I did not get her pregnant. I'm in love with her.' *Ouch. That hurt. Not sure I want to say that again. It might make it happen.*

Perish the thought!

Vittorio gave a disdainful laugh. 'The day you fall in love is the day hell freezes over or I get accepted into heaven. Take your pick; neither of them is going to happen. You don't have the capacity to love. You're exactly like me in that regard. Love is for emotionally weak people who can't survive without being propped up by someone else.'

Remy knew his grandfather was scathing about his brothers for falling in love. He mocked them any chance he could, picking Poppy and Lily to pieces as if they were not real people with feelings but department-store items Rafe and Raoul had picked up that, in Vittorio's opinion, were somehow faulty.

Remy didn't like admitting it but deep down he was starting to feel a little envious of how happy his brothers were. How settled; secure; anchored. His life of flying in and flying out of cities and relationships had always seemed so exciting and satisfying up until now.

He shook off the thought like the snow he'd just brushed off his shoulders. 'Be that as it may, you have to admit she's great to look at. What more could a man ask for than a stunningly beautiful wife who loves him?'

'She's stunning but she's Henri Marchand's daughter. Do you really want to mix your blood with the likes of him?'

What was his grandfather's obsession about babies? It was making Remy distinctly uneasy. 'We're leaving the breeding to Rafe and Raoul. Angelique wants to keep her figure.'

Vittorio grunted. 'She won't stay with you. You mark my words. Next thing you know, she'll slap divorce papers on you and take half your assets. You're a fool to enter a marriage without a pre-nuptial agreement. I thought you had more sense than your brothers. Seems I was wrong.'

It did worry Remy about the lack of a pre-nup but he wasn't going to dwell on it while he had other more pressing matters to deal with. Besides, Angelique had her own reasons for wanting the marriage to continue.

The bridal-wear gig was huge. He'd already seen hundreds of tweets about it. It was amusingly ironic to think of her modelling the one type of outfit she loathed more than any other.

'How's that new housemaid working out?' Remy asked.

'She's got a face like a monkey.'

Remy rolled his eyes. Some things never changed. 'I might pop over in a couple of weeks to see you once I've sorted out a few business issues. I'll bring Angelique with me.'

Vittorio gave another cynical grunt. 'That's if she's still with you by then.'

CHAPTER ELEVEN

ANGELIQUE CAME DOWN to the large sitting room where Remy was stoking a roaring fire. Warmth was spreading throughout the house now the heating was on but the sound of the flames crackling and spitting in the fireplace reminded her of cosy times with her grandparents when she was young.

The removals company had obviously come and taken away her father's personal belongings, leaving just the original furniture. Without Henri's things here it was like stepping back in time to a happier period in her life.

But it still annoyed her that Remy had possession of her family home and was so determined to keep it. It was all very well sleeping with him and fancying herself in love with him, but at the end of the day she had to get her home back.

Her goal was to get the deeds to Tarrantloch back where they belonged. Nothing else was supposed to distract her from that.

Not Remy with his smouldering looks, spine-loosening smile, his magical touch and mind-blowing love-making. She could indulge in an affair with him for the period of their marriage but it had to end with her achieving her mission.

Tarrantloch was meant to be hers and she would not be satisfied until she had it back in her possession.

Remy stood up and glanced at her over his shoulder. 'Warming up?'

'You certainly move fast.' Angelique walked further into the room. 'You've had every trace of my father's occupation of the place removed.'

He kicked a piece of charcoal back into the fire with the side of his shoe before he looked at her again. 'That's normally what a new owner does, is it not?'

Angelique set her jaw. Did he have to rub it in every chance he got? 'What do you plan to do with it?'

'I want to base myself here.' He dusted off his hands from having placed another log on the fire. 'It's private and far enough away from a major city to put off the paparazzi.'

She frowned at him. 'But you're a big city man. You spend most of your time in casinos and clubs. You'd be bored out of your mind up here in the highlands with nothing but the wind and the rain and the snow for company.'

'I don't know about that…' He nudged absently at the fire with the poker. 'Rafe's been raving about the mansion he bought in Oxfordshire—the one that Poppy's grandmother used to work in when she was growing up.' He put the poker back in its holder and faced her again. 'He originally planned to turn it into a luxury hotel for the rich and famous but now he's living there with Poppy. It's home to them now, it's where they plan to bring up a family.'

'That's all very well and good, but you're not a family man,' Angelique pointed out. 'You're going to get lonely up here unless you regularly fly in some party girls to while away the long winter nights.'

He shrugged a shoulder and kicked at another piece of charcoal that had fallen out of the fire. 'It may surprise you, but I don't spend all of my time partying and gambling. That's one of the reasons I love Dharbiri so much. It's so different from the life I live in the city.'

'It's certainly different.' Her tone was wry. 'It's not a place I'm going to forget in a hurry.'

He met her gaze across the glow of the firelight. 'Apart from the sand and the heat it's much the same as here. It has a bleak sort of raw beauty about it. You can hear the silence.'

She gave him a knowing look. 'It might be isolated and a little bleak up here but no one's going to come barging in threatening to flay you alive if you have an unchaperoned woman in your room.'

He acknowledged that with little incline of his head. 'Perhaps not, but I bet there are quaint old ways and customs up here in the highlands and on some of the west coast islands.'

'I still don't think you'll last a winter up here.' Angelique sat down on the sofa and curled her legs underneath her body. 'It can get snowbound for weeks and the wind can bore ice-pick holes in your chest. And don't get me started about the rain in summer. It goes on for weeks at a time. Quite frankly, I don't even know why they bother calling it summer. It should be called the wet season, like in the tropics.' She flicked her hair back behind her shoulders. 'Oh, and did I mention the midges and mosquitoes? They're as big as Clydesdales.'

He crossed one ankle over the other as he leaned against the mantelpiece, a lazy smile curving his lips. 'If it's as bad as you say then why do you love it up here so much?'

She looked at the flickering flames before she answered. 'I spent some of the happiest days of my life up here when I was a child.'

'You came here with your parents?'

'My mother,' Angelique said. 'It was her parents', my grandparents', home. My father never used to come because he was always too busy with work. I think the truth was he didn't get on with my grandparents. They didn't like him. I was too young to remember specific conversations but I got the impression they thought he was two-faced.' She looked back at the fire again. 'They were right. Everything changed when my nanna died. The grief hit my mother hard and then my granddad died less than a year later. It was devastating for my mother. That's when things started to get a little crazy at home.'

Remy was frowning when she looked at him again. 'That's when she became depressed?'

Angelique nodded. 'She must have felt so lonely once her parents were gone. She was shy and lacked confidence, which was probably why my father was attracted to her in the first place. He saw her as someone he could control.'

Remy's frown was more of anger than anything. 'I wish I'd flattened him when I had the chance. What a cowardly son of a bitch.'

'You hurt him far more by taking Tarrantloch off him,' Angelique said. 'And of course by marrying me. That really stung. He won't get over that in a hurry.'

His expression turned rueful. 'Yes, well, my grandfather isn't too happy about it either.'

'You've spoken to him?'

'He called when I was bringing in the bags. And it wasn't to congratulate me.'

'No, I expect not.' She hooked her hands around her

knees. 'I guess the congratulations will come in thick and fast once we divorce.'

The silence was broken only by the hiss and crackle of the flames in the fireplace.

Angelique chanced a glance at him but he was staring into the fire as if it were the most befuddling thing he'd ever seen. Was he worried about their lack of a pre-nup? It was certainly a worrying thing for a man with wealth—or a woman, for that matter—to be exposed to the possibility of a financial carve-up in the event of a divorce.

The only way to avoid it would be to *stay* married.

Which was not something Remy would be likely to suggest, even to keep control of his fortune. He didn't do love and commitment. He was the epitome of the freedom-loving playboy. Tying him down would be like trying to tame a lion with a toothpick.

It wasn't going to happen.

Remy turned from the fire. 'I don't suppose there's any point in asking if you're hungry?'

Angelique unhooked her hands from around her legs. 'I am, actually. It must be the cold wintry air. I used to eat heaps when I came here as a kid. My nanna was a fabulous cook.'

'Your grandparents didn't have a housekeeper?'

'Yes, but nanna still did most of the cooking. I used to help her. I can still make a mean batch of oat cakes and flapjacks.'

He smiled a sexy smile as he held out his hand to her. 'I'm told it can sometimes get very hot in the kitchen.'

Angelique felt a tingle in her core as his strong fingers wrapped around hers. She gave him a sultry look. 'If you think it's going to be too hot for you, then you should stay out of there.'

He brought her up against his body, his *aroused* body. Another tingle coursed through her, making her nipples stand to attention. His gaze zeroed in on her mouth for a pulsing beat. 'I'm pretty sure I can handle it.'

She moved against him, just the once, but it made his eyes go almost black with desire. 'You think?'

He swept her up in his arms and carried her towards the door. 'Let's go and find out.'

Remy slid her down his body once they got to the kitchen. Her body inflamed his; he had been burning for her ever since they'd arrived. It seemed years since he'd last made love with her but it had only been last night. And what a night that had been.

He craved her.

Ached for her.

His groin was tight with longing; he wanted to sink into her and lose himself. Block his thoughts—the rational, sensible ones, that was. He wanted to feel the magic of her touch, the way her body clenched so tightly around him as if she never wanted to let him go. He could not remember a more passionate, exciting lover. It felt different somehow...more intense; as if his skin had developed a new, overly sensitive layer that only responded to her touch.

Remy started playing with her lower lip in little tug-and-release bites. 'How's the heat so far?'

She snaked her arms up around his neck and threaded her fingers through his hair. 'Not hot enough.' She slid her tongue into his mouth and he nearly disgraced himself then and there.

He took control of the kiss, deepening the thrusts of his tongue as it chased and subdued hers. She gave little gasps and encouraging groans, her body pressing as close as she physically could. He felt her mound rubbing against his erection, a tantalising tease of the delights to come.

He lifted her up on to the kitchen bench and stood between her spread thighs. 'You're wearing too many clothes,' he growled against her mouth.

She nibbled at his lips. 'That would be because it's below freezing outside.'

He grabbed at the back of his cashmere sweater and tugged it over his head. Next came his shirt, which lost a button or two in the process. 'Now let's start on you.'

She gave him a seductive look as she undid the tiny pearl buttons of her designer cardigan. She was wearing a black lacy camisole underneath that showed the shadow of her cleavage and the perfect globes of her breasts. 'I'm not wearing a bra.'

His groin tightened another notch. 'I can see that.'

She peeled the shoestring straps over her shoulders, one by one, lowering the lacy garment slowly, like a high-class stripper. 'You want to touch me, don't you?'

I want to do more than touch you. 'What gives you that idea?' Remy did his deadpan face.

Her lips curved upwards in a siren's smile. 'I'm not going to let you touch me until I'm good and ready. You have to be a good boy and wait.' She lowered her camisole a little further, revealing a tightly budded pink nipple. 'Do you think you can do that?'

Remy had to count backwards to stop himself from jumping the gun. His need was pulsating with such relentless force it was painful. 'I'll wait, but you do realise at some point in the future you're going to pay for this, don't you?'

She gave a little mock shiver. 'Ooh! Is that supposed to scare me?'

'Be scared,' he growled. 'Be very scared.'

She exposed her other breast, all the while holding his gaze with the dancing, mischievous heat of hers. She glided her hand down over her belly to the waist-band of her pencil-thin designer jeans. 'I'm wet. I bet you want to feel how wet, don't you?'

Remy had never been so turned on. He was fighting to keep his hands off her. He couldn't think about any-thing but the need to thrust into her to the hilt and ex-plode. 'I'm hard. I bet you want to feel how hard, huh?'

Her eyes sparkled as she traced a fingertip down the ridge of his erection through the fabric of his trousers. 'Mmm; impressive.' She took the same fingertip and traced it down the denim-covered seam of her body. 'I guess I should get out of my jeans. Would you like that?'

I would love that. 'Take your time.'

She slithered down off the bench, pushing him back with a fingertip. 'Not so close, big boy. You don't get to touch until I give the go ahead.'

Remy mentally gulped. This was going to end badly if she didn't speed things up a bit. He could feel his erection straining against his jeans. He just hoped the fabric was strong enough to hold him in.

She was definitely going to pay for this.

And it would involve a leather whip and handcuffs.

Angelique locked gazes with him and slowly undid her zipper. The sound of it going down was magnified in the throbbing silence. She stepped out of her heels and then she peeled the jeans off her legs. Once they were off she stepped back into her heels, leaving just the black lace of her knickers on. 'So…' She ran the tip of her tongue over her lower lip leaving it wet and glis-tening. 'Are you getting excited?'

Way, way beyond that. 'What do you think?'

She traced his erection again, her eyes still holding his in a sexy little lock that made his blood heat to boiling. 'How badly do you want me?'

Off the scale. 'Let's put it this way. Right now I could do you in five seconds flat.'

Her eyes flared and then her lips pushed forwards in a pout. 'That sounds like I would be left high and dry.'

'Don't worry. I'd take you along for the ride.'

She put that teasing fingertip to work again. 'What if I was to strike up a little deal with you?'

Remy marvelled at her self-control. He'd always thought he was a master at keeping his desire under his command but she had pushed him to the very limit. His body was a mass of twitching nerve endings and primal urgings. But he was still in enough control—only just—to recognise manipulation when he saw it. 'What sort of deal?'

She slowly lowered his zipper. 'A deal where we both get what we want.'

He sucked in a breath as her fingers tugged his underwear aside. It was hard to think straight when she was touching him, stroking him to the very edge, but he was not going to be tricked or manoeuvred into giving away what he had spent years fighting to gain.

Besides, he hadn't just done it for himself: he had done it for his brothers. It wasn't his prize to give away. It represented far more than a victory over a double-crossing enemy. Taking ownership of Tarrantloch was finally setting right the wrongs of the past. Handing it over to the sole heir of the man who had almost destroyed his family's fortune was the very last thing he would consider doing, no matter what his relationship with Angelique was. Or wasn't.

He pushed her hand away and stepped back from her.

'Game over, *ma belle*. I'm not giving you Tarrantloch in exchange for a quick screw up against the kitchen bench. I'm not *that* desperate.'

Her expression switched from sexy siren to outraged virago within a heartbeat. 'You bastard.'

'*Orphan* is the correct term.'

She came at him then like a spitting cat, all claws, snarls and scratches. 'I hate you!'

Remy restrained her by holding both of her flailing arms behind her back, which rather delightfully pushed her pelvis into blistering contact with his. 'You don't hate me. You want me.'

Her grey-blue eyes flashed venom at him. 'Why won't you give me what I want?'

He ripped her knickers down with a ruthless jerk of his hand. 'What do you want the most?' He probed her folds with his painfully erect penis. 'Tell me. Right now, what do you want the most?'

He heard her swallow as he made contact with her slippery moistness. 'I want what's rightfully mine.'

'Then at least we're on the same page,' he said and then he sealed her mouth roughly with his.

Angelique lost herself in his kiss. To be truthful she had lost herself the day she had flown to Dharbiri. Remy had taken control of not just the situation, but also her life and perhaps even her destiny. He had introduced passion and excitement to her and now there was no going back. She didn't want to go back.

How was she going to live without this rush of excitement every time his mouth met with hers?

She had thought she would play him at his own game: up the stakes, tantalise him, tease him until he gave in, but he had turned her efforts around to his advantage.

He was not going to be hoodwinked out of relinquishing Tarrantloch. Nothing she did or offered was going to change his mind.

Tarrantloch was his talisman of success.

His only weakness that she could see was that he wanted her. But even that need was under his tight control. She had ramped up his desire to the point where she thought he would agree to anything.

But it seemed she was the one who was the more desperate.

His mouth was hard against hers but she worked at softening it with little pull-backs and strokes of her tongue. Once he'd eased off a bit she nipped at his lower lip with her teeth, and then laved it with the glide of her tongue.

She felt him rummaging around for a condom, his hands leaving her in order to apply it, but his mouth didn't budge from plundering hers.

He was at her entrance and nudging to possess her. She opened her legs and stood up on tiptoe to welcome him. He surged so thickly and so forcefully she felt her back bump the bench behind. He set a furious pace but her body was so wet, and aching so much, it was a blessed and welcome assault of her senses to feel him pumping so hard. She came almost immediately, not even needing the coaxing stroke of his fingers. All it took was a little roll and tilt of her pelvis and she was flying off into the stratosphere, screaming and sobbing all the way.

He didn't waste time waiting for her to come back to earth. He rocketed after her with a deep, primal grunt as he unloaded. She felt the rise of goose bumps over his back as she held him against her, his hectic breathing a harsh sound in the silence.

Angelique wanted to hate him for turning the tables on her but somehow she couldn't access that emotion right now. So instead she held him and stroked her hands over his back and shoulders, planting soft little teasing kisses to his neck and behind his earlobes.

He eased back from her but only so he could rest his forehead against hers. Their breaths mingled intimately in the space between their mouths. 'I wasn't too rough, was I?' His voice sounded gruff, almost apologetic.

Angelique trailed a fingertip over his bottom lip. 'I wanted you any way I could have you.'

His dark gaze meshed with hers. 'You really turn me on like no other woman I've ever been with, but I have a feeling but you already know that.'

She smiled a little smile and did another circuit with her finger, this time pushing it into his mouth so he could suck on it. It sent a shudder down her spine when he did. His mouth was hot and moist, and his tongue a sexy rasp against her soft skin. When she pulled it out she said in a voice that wasn't quite even. 'You do a pretty fine job of lighting my fire too.'

He held her gaze for an interminable moment. 'We should do something about a meal. I don't want you fading away on me. I have plans for you and, believe me, you're going to need your stamina.'

She traced each of his eyebrows in turn, a playful smile pushing up the corners of her mouth. 'When you look at me like that, I get a wobbly feeling in my girly bits.'

His eyes glinted dangerously as he tugged her back against him. 'And so you damn well should,' he said and brought his mouth down to hers.

CHAPTER TWELVE

REMY WATCHED AS Angelique slept in the tumble of sheets, pillows and bedcoverings that had become their love-making nest over the last three weeks. He had extended their stay because a sudden snowfall had made it impossible for Robert Mappleton to get to their meeting so Remy had to postpone it until the roads cleared.

And what a time it had been.

He and Angelique had made love not just in the bedroom but the bathroom and the sofa in the sitting room; the morning room; the linen room; the utilities room and the kitchen four or five times over. Angelique had delighted him, shocked him, teased and tantalised him until he only had to look at her and his body would swell with lust.

He had lit a fire in the master bedroom. The flickering flames were casting their usual golden glow over the room. There was another fluttering of snow outside; he could see it falling silently past the windows in ghostly handfuls. It had been snowing on and off for a couple of days now but the roads were open again. He felt a niggling sense of disappointment as he had secretly harboured a fantasy of being snowed in with her for weeks on end. Maybe right up to and including Christmas.

Every couple of days they had driven to the village

to buy supplies at the local store. He liked the normality of it, the hunting and gathering that was an everyday occurrence for most people. Angelique knew a few of the locals and had stopped and chatted to them, introducing him as her husband with a naturalness that made him feel like a fraud. If she felt the same way, she showed no sign of it.

Robert Mappleton had left by helicopter that afternoon after an overnight stay. Angelique had shown the class and grace he had come to expect from her. It seemed she could be whatever he wanted or needed her to be: a playful, adventurous lover; an intrepid hiker across the moors or through the forest; a gourmet cook in the kitchen and an engaging, convivial hostess. She had made the old man feel at home, plying him with fabulous home-cooked food and old-fashioned highland hospitality. Mappleton had been charmed—besotted would have been closer to the mark. He had spent most of the time chatting to Angelique and had only given Remy his attention—and cursorily, at that—to sign the papers to hand over the Mappleton chain for a princely sum.

Remy knew he should be feeling happy. Proud. Satisfied. Victorious.

But his mind was restless.

It was time to put an end to this madness but Angelique had a photo shoot lined up in Paris the following day to kick-start her new modelling career. He could hardly walk out on her when so much was at stake for her. As least modelling bridal wear would be better for her than swimwear. There would be less pressure on her to be rail-thin all the time. Over the last few days he had noticed her eating a little more than usual. It had delighted him to see her enjoy her food instead of seeing it as an enemy.

Talking of enemies...

He was having more and more trouble thinking of her as an opponent. He looked at her lying next to him; at the way the light fell on her cheekbone as she was lying with her head resting on one of her hands. She looked so peaceful. Relaxed and sated.

He felt a little free-fall inside his stomach as he recalled the way she had crawled all over him earlier that night. His body was still humming with the aftershocks of having her ride him.

Was there no end to this driving lust he felt for her? He kept waiting to feel that flat feeling of boredom, the tinge of irritation that nearly always occurred about now in his relationships. He would look at the woman in his bed and wonder: *what was I thinking?*

But when he looked at Angelique in his bed, he thought: *how can I keep her there?*

Angelique made a sleepy sound from the tangle of sheets and then opened her eyes. 'What time is it?'

'Late. Or early. I guess it depends on whether you're a night owl or a lark.'

She sat up and pushed her dark hair back over her naked shoulders. 'I'm not sure what I am any more. I think I've crossed too many time zones or something.'

Remy pushed himself away from the mantelpiece. 'I'm cooking breakfast this morning. I think it's time you had a break from the kitchen.'

Her brows lifted. 'Wonders will never cease. I never thought I'd see the day when you put on an apron.'

He grinned at her. 'Not only that, I actually picked up a towel and hung it back on the rack. How's that for becoming domesticated?'

She gave him a beady look. 'Toilet seat?'

'Down.'

She gave a slow smile. 'Wow. That's pretty impressive. Maybe there's hope for you as a husband after all. Some girl in the future is really going to thank me for training you.' She tapped her finger against her lips musingly. 'Maybe I should think about opening a school for future husbands. There could be a big market for that: *give me your man and I'll whip him into shape.* What do you think?'

'Did you say *whip*?'

'I meant that metaphorically.'

'Pity.'

Her eyes danced with mischief and his blood raced. 'You don't really want me to beat you, do you?' she asked.

He came over to the bed and tipped up her chin with the end of his finger. 'I sometimes wonder if I'll ever know the real you. You're full of surprises.'

Her look was all sexy siren. 'Who do you want me to be?'

He dropped his hand from her chin. He felt strangely dissatisfied by her answer. He was all for playing games when it suited him, but he wanted to *know* her: the *real* Angelique Marchand. What she felt and thought and believed in. What she valued.

Who she loved.

It was ironic but in many ways she reminded him of himself. She had forged a reputation for herself as scatty and irresponsible, as a wild tearaway who had no intention of putting down roots. She had shied away from commitment like he did. She had hated the thought of the formality and entrapment of marriage. She was a free spirit who wanted to live and enjoy life on her terms.

But was that who she really was? Or was it what she thought people expected her to be?

Remy tried to think of another girl who would be in his bed in the flickering firelight some time in the future and couldn't quite do it. He kept seeing Angelique with her fragrant cloud of dark hair, her arresting grey-blue eyes and her bee-stung mouth with its lush, kiss-me ripeness…

He gave himself a mental shake.

He wasn't interested in a future with her. He wasn't interested in a future with anyone.

He was interested in the here and now.

Today and tomorrow were his only focus.

He didn't want to think any further ahead.

Angelique swung her legs over the edge of the bed, but as she stood up she tottered for a moment and went a ghastly shade of white. He put out a hand to steady her. 'Are you all right?'

She looked a little dazed for a moment or two but then her colour slowly returned. 'Whoa, that was strange. I thought I was going to faint. It's not like I've not been eating enough. I still feel full from all that chocolate pudding I had last night.'

He pushed a tiny tendril of hair back from her face. 'Maybe I've been keeping you up too late.'

She smiled cheekily as she danced her fingertips down his bare forearm. He felt the electric shock of her touch all the way to his groin. 'I'm the one who's been keeping you up.'

He was up right now—painfully so. But she was still looking peaky even if she was putting on a brave front. He knew that about her if nothing else. She was excellent at hiding behind various masks. He gently patted her on the behind. 'Have your shower while I rustle up some breakfast. How does bacon and eggs sound?'

The colour drained from her face again and she quickly thrust a hand to her mouth and bolted for the *en suite*. Remy followed her to find her hunched over the toilet seat, retching without actually bringing anything up. 'Oh, *ma petite*, why didn't you say you were feeling sick?' he said.

She wiped her mouth on the face cloth he handed her. 'I didn't feel sick until you mentioned… Urgh.' She gave a little shudder. 'I'm not even going to say the words.'

'Shall I call a doctor?'

'What on earth for?' She got to her feet and grabbed her hair and, using its length, tied it in a loose knot behind her head. 'It's just a stomach bug. I've had them before. It'll pass in twenty-four hours or so.'

He reached for her forehead but it was clammy rather than hot. 'Do you want to go back to bed?'

She pushed his hand away, a little frown creasing her forehead. 'Stop fussing, Remy. I'm fine.'

'You look pale.'

'I haven't got my make-up on.'

'Personally, I prefer you without it.' He followed her back into the bedroom. 'Are you sure you don't want me to call a doctor?'

'And make me look like a drama queen for dragging him or her out here to diagnose a virus? No thanks.'

Remy pulled back the covers on the bed. 'In. Rest for an hour and see how you feel.'

She rolled her eyes and flopped back down on the bed. 'You should keep well away from me. It might be catching.'

'I'll risk it.'

'I should probably warn you, I'm not a very good nurse. I have no patience or compassion.'

He smiled as he touched her cheek with a lazy finger. 'I think you'd make a very good nurse. You'd look hot in a uniform too.'

She cranked one eye open. 'I thought you preferred me without clothes?'

He gave her hand a gentle squeeze. 'Right now I'd prefer you to rest up. We have to get you to Paris in tip-top shape.'

'And after Paris?'

'We have Raoul and Lily's wedding.'

A little frown pulled at her brow. 'Are you sure I should go to that?'

'I want you there.' He meant it, which was a little surprising. Worrying, actually. He had to let her go at some point; no point dragging this on too long.

'But I thought once your business deal with Robert Mappleton was done we were going to go our separate ways.'

Remy searched her gaze but he wasn't sure what he was looking for. 'It would look a bit suspicious if we parted within a day or two of the contract being signed. And your manager is going to be pretty pissed with you if you suddenly announce you're getting a divorce. I think we should leave things as they are until after Raoul and Lily's wedding. It's only a matter of weeks. We can reassess things in the New Year.'

'What have you told your brothers about us? Surely they know the truth?'

'Yes, but that's not the point. I don't want a big press fest on our break-up occurring right in the middle of Raoul and Lily's wedding.'

Remy had spoken to Raoul not long after Rafe had

called. But, rather than berate him for marrying Angelique, he had said what his grandfather had said—that he'd always sensed Remy had a thing for her and that his little spin about her being hell on heels didn't ring true with him. It had annoyed Remy to think he hadn't disguised his feelings as well as he'd thought. What would Raoul make of his feelings now?

Angelique's gaze narrowed. 'You're not falling in love with me, are you?'

He coughed out a laugh. 'Are you joking? I've never fallen in love in my life.'

'Good.' She closed her eyes again. 'I don't want any hearts broken when this is over.'

Remy got up from the bed. 'I'll come and check on you in an hour.'

'I'll be back in the ring and punching by then.'

'I'll look forward to it.'

He walked to the door but when he turned back to look at her she had turned her back and was huddled into a tight ball.

Something shifted in his chest: a slippage; a gear not quite meshing with its cogs.

He shook off the feeling and walked out, closing the door softly behind him.

Angelique rolled over to her back, pressing a hand to her churning stomach. She was due for a period. She had taken herself off the pill months ago because she felt the brand she'd been on was making her put on weight. She hadn't bothered renewing her prescription because she hadn't been dating anyone. But she didn't feel period pain, just this wretched, churning nausea. That near-faint had happened a few times before when she hadn't eaten enough. But she could hardly use the lack of food as an excuse because she had been eating normally over the last couple of weeks. The thought of not having to bare her body all the time in a bikini was like being let out of prison. She was almost getting excited about the Paris shoot. Almost.

She swung her legs over the edge of the bed again and tested her balance. So far so good. Her stomach was uneasy but her head was more or less clear. She padded back to the bathroom and stepped into the shower. She closed her eyes as the water cascaded down and mentally calculated when her last period had been—was it four weeks or five?

She was occasionally overdue; disruptions came with the stress of dieting and travelling.

Anyway, they'd used condoms. The failure rate was miniscule…but enough to be slightly worrying. Terrifyingly worrying.

Angelique put a hand to her concave belly. It wasn't possible. She wasn't the type of girl to get herself pregnant. It just couldn't happen.

She thought of the first time when Remy had taken for ever to withdraw. Had some of his Olympic-strong swimmers sneaked out past the barrier of the condom and gone in search of one of her desperate little eggs?

Oh, traitorous body and even more traitorous hormones!

Panic set in. She felt it clutch at her insides. She felt it move over her skin like a clammy shiver. She felt it hammering in her chest.

She couldn't be pregnant. *She couldn't be.*

Buying a pregnancy test in a village this small was out of the question. She would have to wait until she got to Paris. And then after Paris, baby or no baby, she would have to attend Raoul and Lily's wedding and pretend everything was normal in front of their family and friends. It seemed so tacky to be attending a romantic wedding when theirs had been so extravagant yet so meaningless.

Angelique felt a pang of envy for Raoul's bride-to-be, Lily. How excited she must be getting prepared for her wedding. Doing all the girly things to make her day so special. Angelique cringed when she thought of her wedding to Remy. The whole thing had been nothing but a big, overblown sham. She was a fraud. A fake bride. A fake wife. And this was a fake honeymoon.

If she was pregnant would Remy insist on her staying with him for the sake of the child? He would end up hating her for tying him down. He might even end up hating the child.

Angelique bit her lip as she looked in the mirror at her body. For years she had denied her body, punished her body, controlled her body, but now it would not just be hers but the shelter in which her baby—hers and Remy's baby—would grow and develop.

She could not think of getting rid of it. It was certainly an option and one she felt other women were entitled to make. But it wasn't for her.

She put a hand to her flat belly. How could it be possible that she and Remy had made a baby? He didn't even like her.

Well, maybe that wasn't quite true. He certainly didn't hate her any more. She had seen him looking at her with lust, longing, amusement, and even annoyance when she got in the last word, but not hatred.

Their relationship had changed over the last three weeks. They still bickered occasionally but it was a sort of foreplay. They were both strong-willed and determined and didn't like losing an argument or debate.

It was foolish of her to have fallen in love with him

but it had happened so long ago it was pointless flagellating herself about it now. She had fallen in love with him at the age of fifteen.

She still remembered the day it had happened. She had gone with her father to Vittorio's villa for a function. Remy had been home for a visit and he'd been assigned the task of keeping her entertained while her father and Vittorio had a business meeting before dinner. She had been waiting in the home entertainment room, idly leafing through one of her fashion magazines, when Remy had come in. She hadn't seen him in a year or two. Her heart had quite literally stopped when he had come in. He had been so tall and so staggeringly handsome, with that lazy smile that had travelled all the way to his eyes.

But as soon as she had stood up his smile had disappeared. He'd seemed a little taken aback seeing her dressed in a short denim skirt and a clinging top that revealed a generous amount of cleavage due to the brandnew push-up bra she'd bought.

He had cleared his throat, walked briskly over to the television, selected a movie and set it running. 'There, that should keep you happy for a while.'

'I'm not twelve,' she'd said with a pout.

He'd pushed a hand through his thick overly long hair. 'It's a good movie. It won two Oscar nomination and three Golden Globes.'

She had put on her beseeching face. 'Will you watch it with me?'

He had muttered something that sounded very much like an English swear word before he had sat down on the sofa furthest away from her. But he had stayed and watched it with her. He'd even laughed at the funny bits, and at one point paused the movie to go and get some popcorn he'd charmed one of the housemaids to make.

Yes, falling in love with him had been the easy bit.

Falling out of love was going to be the kicker.

CHAPTER THIRTEEN

'ARE YOU SURE you're all right?' Remy asked Angelique when they landed in Paris. 'You've been so quiet and you still look a little pale.'

'I'm fine.' She gave him a tight smile. 'I'm just nervous. The thought of all those wedding dresses is enough to make my insides churn.'

He put an arm around her waist as they walked out to the waiting car. 'You'll blow everyone away as soon as you walk up that aisle.'

Angelique hadn't been sick for the last couple of days but she still felt queasy in the stomach. She had managed to keep it from Remy but then saw a pharmacy ahead and wondered how she could sneak in and get a testing kit without him noticing. But just then his phone rang and she seized the opportunity. She pointed to the ladies' room and mouthed the words to him about needing to take a pit stop. He nodded and turned away, plugging one ear so he could hear the conversation without all the noise of the busy airport terminal.

Angelique walked briskly into the shop and bought tampons—that was her positive thinking working overtime—and a pregnancy kit. She put both items in her tote bag and came out with her heart thumping so loudly she could feel it in her throat.

Remy was still talking on the phone and only turned around when she appeared by his side. He ended the call and slipped his arm back around her waist. 'That was Robert Mappleton. He said to say hi.'

'He's a very nice man,' Angelique said, falling in step beside him as they made their way out to the waiting car. 'He really misses his wife. She died eight years ago after a long struggle with breast cancer. They'd been married for forty-nine years. She used to do a lot of the background work in the business. I think that's why it went downhill so badly. He's been grieving all this time.'

Remy glanced down at her. 'He told you all that?'

She nodded. 'We talked about the grieving process—the denial, the anger, the bargaining, transition and then acceptance. I told him how lost I'd felt when my mother died. He was very understanding. He and his wife couldn't have children.' She gave a little sigh. 'Wouldn't it be cool if we could choose our parents? I would've loved a father like Robert Mappleton instead of my own.'

Remy's arm tightened protectively. 'I wish I could have mine back, just for a day, to tell him how much he meant to me. And my mother.'

Angelique leaned against his shoulder. 'They'd be very proud of you and your brothers.'

His expression clouded and he looked away. 'Of Rafe and Raoul maybe, but me? I'm not so sure.'

'But why? You've just nailed the biggest deal of your career. It's bigger than anything your brothers have done.'

He looked at her again. It was a hard look: cynical; jaded. 'It's just another deal.' He dropped his arm from her waist and took her hand instead. 'Come on. We'd better get you to the church on time.'

Remy stood at the back of the photo shoot in one of Paris's gothic cathedrals as Angelique was photographed in a variety of bridal outfits. She looked stunning in every one of them. It made him think of their wedding back in Dharbiri. She had looked fabulous then too, but nothing about that day had been real.

He couldn't help imagining her as a real bride, walking down the aisle not to a crowd of photographers but to him.

He blinked and shook his head. It was definitely too hot and stuffy in here or something.

He looked back at the action playing out in front of him. The photographers, all six of them, issued commands and directions, which Angelique followed tirelessly like the consummate professional she was. Her manager had come over and introduced herself earlier, telling him how Angelique's star was set to shine brighter than any model she had represented before.

Remy felt proud of Angelique in a way he had never quite expected to feel. He had always thought her spoilt and wilful, yet seeing how she treated the more junior staff on the shoot with respect and kindness made him realise he had seriously misjudged her.

You're falling for her.

No, I'm not.

Yes, you are. Big time.

Remy's phone vibrated in his pocket but instead of ignoring it he welcomed the distraction. He didn't even check the screen to see who was calling as he stepped outside the cathedral to answer it. 'Remy Caffarelli.'

'I want you and your brothers here tomorrow for a family meeting,' Vittorio said.

Typical. His grandfather always expected everyone to dance around him at a moment's notice. Remy would go when he was good and ready and not before. 'I can't drop everything just because you fancy a family get-together.'

'Where are you?'

'In Paris with Angelique. She's working.'

'She wouldn't know how to work unless it was flat on her back.'

Anger tightened every muscle in Remy's spine. 'That's my wife you're insulting. I won't have you or anyone speak about her like that.'

'If you don't come here tomorrow I'll tell the press your marriage to that little black-haired slut is nothing but a sham.'

Remy felt a cold hand of dread grab at his guts. It wasn't the deal with Robert Mappleton he was most worried about. What would happen to Angelique's new-found career if that sort of leak got out before her first shoot was even over?

How on earth had Vittorio found out? His brothers would never have betrayed him. He had sworn them to secrecy.

There could only be one person who would want to do the dirty on him even if it hurt his only daughter in the process.

Henri Marchand.

Angelique came over to where Remy was standing at the back of the church once her shoot was over for the day. 'I didn't expect you to stay the whole time. You must be bored out of your brain. There's nothing more tediously boring than watching mascara dry— Hey, is something wrong? Why are you frowning like that? Are you cross with me?'

Remy forcibly relaxed his frown. 'Sorry, *ma petite*. It's not you. It's my grandfather. He's insisting on a family meeting tomorrow. He won't take no for an answer. Can you ask for a day off? I know it's short notice.'

She frowned at him. 'He wants *me* there? But why?'

'I'll explain it later. I don't want anyone listening in. Do you think you can get tomorrow off?'

'I'm sure it'll be fine. There's been a delay on the next collection. Mackenzie just told me about it. We're shooting at a private château in Vichy the day after tomorrow so I'm all yours till then.'

Remy put his arm around her shoulders and hugged her close. 'Best news I've had all day.'

Angelique didn't have time to do anything about the pregnancy test because Remy had organised a flight straight to Rome. She tried to put her worries to the back of her mind. She was probably imagining her symptoms anyway. Stress always made her stomach churn. And being late with a period was certainly not unusual; it came with the territory of dieting and travelling across time zones.

And, to be fair, Remy had been keeping her up late at night, not that she was complaining. The nights in his arms were the highlight of her day. Not that he had restricted their passionate interludes to the evenings: mornings, mid-morning, lunchtimes, afternoons and evenings had been spent in a variety of activities that had made every cell in her body shudder with delight.

It worried her that it might soon be over. His deal was done and dusted. The only thing keeping them together was her modelling contract—a contract she didn't even want.

Rafe and Poppy arrived just as they were getting out of the car at Vittorio's villa, so there was no chance of slipping away and finding out one way or the other about the result.

Rafe was distinctly cool with Angelique but Poppy was anything but. She wrapped her arms around Angelique and gave her a warm hug. 'It's so lovely to meet you.' She pulled back to look at her. 'Oh. My. God. You're *so* beautiful! I'm having such a fan moment. I feel I should be asking for your autograph or something.'

Angelique loved her already. 'Congratulations on your marriage.' It was the first thing she thought of to say.

Poppy's toffee-brown eyes twinkled. 'Congratulations on yours.' She leaned in close so the boys couldn't hear. 'And all that rubbish about it being a sham just to save your necks doesn't fool me for a second.'

Angelique quickly schooled her features. She wasn't ready to play confidante just yet, even if Poppy was the sort of girl she longed to have as a best friend. 'Sorry to burst your bubble, but I'm not in love with him. We're just making the most of being stuck together. I've always fancied him, but then what girl with a pulse wouldn't?'

'Oh, well…sorry. I just thought… Never mind.' Poppy's flustered look was replaced with a smile. 'Just wait until you meet Lily, Raoul's fiancée. She's a darling. She's quite shy but once you get to know her I'm sure you'll adore her.'

'I'm not worried about Lily or Raoul,' Angelique

said. 'It's Vittorio I'm concerned with. I've always been a little terrified of him.'

Poppy rolled her eyes. 'Tell me about it. I avoid him as much as possible. So do Rafe and Raoul. I think Remy is the only one who can crack a smile out of him. But you know him, don't you? Rafe told me you used to come here a lot when your father and Vittorio were business partners.'

'Yes, but it was a long time ago, and there's been a lot of dirty water under the bridge since then.'

Poppy gave her a friendly smile. 'Maybe, but you weren't the one to put it there. Now, let's go and meet Lily and Raoul. That's their car arriving. See?'

Angelique watched as a slim ash-brown-haired young woman stepped out of the car to go around to the driver's side with a pair of crutches. 'I thought Raoul couldn't walk any more?'

'He can take a few steps now,' Poppy said. 'Lily's been amazing for him. They're just the most adorable couple. Check out the way he looks at her. It just makes me melt.'

Angelique felt an ache around her heart when she saw Raoul take the crutches from Lily. He smiled a smile that was so much more than a smile. It was the smile of a man hopelessly in love. But when she looked at Lily she saw the same thing: Lily was besotted with Raoul and was not one bit ashamed about showing it.

They came over to where the rest of them were standing. Raoul leaned heavily on his crutches to offer a hand to Angelique. 'Welcome to the family, Angelique. It's good to have you here again. It's been a long time. Too long.'

Angelique felt a sudden rush of emotion. Raoul had

always been the nicest to her. '*Merci.* I'm sorry about your accident. I sent a card. Did you get it?'

He gave her a warm smile. 'It meant a lot to me. It made me smile, which I wasn't doing a lot of back then.' He rebalanced on his crutches so he could get Lily to step forward. '*Ma chérie*, this is Angelique, an old family friend and now Remy's wife. Angelique, this is my fiancée, Lily Archer.'

Angelique took Lily's hand. 'I'm very pleased to meet you.'

'And you,' Lily said with a shy smile. 'Wow, you really are as stunning as you are on those billboards and in those magazines.'

'You should see me before breakfast,' Angelique said. 'I spend a fortune on cover-up and I'm on a constant diet. How I look is totally fake.' *I'm a fake.*

Lily's smile said she didn't believe it for a second. 'Maybe you could give me some make-up tips for my wedding. I'm not very good at that stuff.'

'I would be happy to. You have amazing blue eyes. They're so incredibly dark. Has anyone ever told you that?'

Lily smiled and glanced at Raoul who was looking at her with such a tender look it made Angelique's heart suddenly contract. 'Yes; yes, they have. Many times.'

There was a rumble from inside the villa like a dragon emerging from his cave. Vittorio suddenly appeared at the front door with a savage frown between his brows as his gaze fell on Angelique. 'I always knew you'd be trouble. You're just like your two-faced father.'

Angelique stepped forward with her shoulders back and her chin at a combative height. 'I don't think it's fair that I should be judged for the wrongs my father did to you and your family. I had nothing to do with it. I'm an innocent party.'

Vittorio glared at her. 'There's not too much about you that's innocent.'

Angelique stared him down. 'Yes, well, perhaps there's some truth in that, given what your grandson has been doing with me over the last three or four weeks.'

'You shameless hussy!' Vittorio spat at her. 'I bet your double-dealing father put you up to this. No wonder he couldn't wait to crow about it when he called me the other day. You tricked Remy into marrying you so you could carve up his assets when you bail out of it.'

Remy stepped up and put an arm around Angelique's waist. 'I've already warned you about speaking about or to Angelique in a disrespectful manner. She is my wife, and you will treat her with the respect accorded to that position.'

Vittorio curled his top lip. 'How long are you going to keep her? She's not going to stay with you. She'll do the dirty on you first chance she gets. You've left yourself wide open. She's a witch. A Jezebel. You're crazy to think she's going to stick by you. She'll take half of what you own because you've been thinking with your—'

'I'm not taking anything that isn't rightly mine,' Angelique said.

Vittorio laughed. 'Do you think my grandson will hand that castle over just because you opened your legs for him? He's not that much of a fool. His winning that property off your father was the one time I felt proud to call him my grandson. He won't relinquish a prize like that. He's too much like me to give in just because a beautiful woman bats her eyelashes at him.'

'That's enough!' Remy barked. 'Stop it right there.'

Poppy came to the rescue. 'I think it's time for us

girls to get to know one another over some devil's food cake, which strangely enough seems rather appropriate just now. You boys can have your family meeting. We want no part of it.'

Lily touched Angelique's hand. 'Maybe this would be a good time to swap make-up tips.'

'You could be right,' Angelique said.

Rafe took Remy aside after Vittorio had stormed off in a temper. 'You OK?'

Remy clenched and unclenched his fists. 'I swear to God I could have punched him for that.'

'Yes, well, maybe you're feeling hot under the collar because there's a bit of truth in what he said.'

Remy glared at his brother. 'Don't you start. I'm nothing like him.'

Rafe gave him his 'older and wiser' look. 'We're all a bit like him, Remy. There's no point trying to hide from it. It's best to face it and deal with it. We've all used people to get what we want. We've learned it off him. But it doesn't mean we have to go on being like that. I know I've always taught you and Raoul to set goals and to focus, but I've come to realise that winning at any cost is not always the right or the wisest thing to do.'

'I know what I'm doing.' Remy tightened his jaw. 'I don't need your advice or guidance any more.'

Rafe gave his shoulder a squeeze. 'Sorry. I have this lifetime habit of feeling responsible for you. You're old enough to make your own decisions.'

And take full responsibility for them, Remy thought.

'Is Angelique all right?' Raoul asked as he came over once Rafe had left to join Poppy and the girls. 'She looked really pale and fragile. You haven't been giving her a hard time, have you?'

Remy slid his brother a look. 'Trust you to be the softie. She's fine. She's had a stomach bug and the shoot she was on yesterday was long and tiring.'

'What's going on with you two? Is it true what she said to *Nonno*?'

'You know what Angelique's like,' Remy said. 'She likes centre stage. The bigger the scene she makes, the better.'

Raoul's mouth tightened in reproach. 'She's a nice kid, Remy. I've always thought so. A bit messed up because of her mother dying so young and all, but she's a got a good heart. Just because she's got an asshole for a father isn't her fault. She didn't screw us over. Henri did.'

'And I got him back,' Remy said through tight lips.

'Yes, by taking the one thing Angelique loves above everything else.' Raoul readjusted his crutches under his arms. 'You should give Tarrantloch back to her. It doesn't belong to you, bet or no bet. It belongs to her.'

'How do you know I wasn't planning to do that once our marriage comes to an end?'

Raoul gave him a levelling look. 'That's some parting gift, bro. But have you considered she might not want it to end?'

Remy gave a short bark of cynical laughter. 'Can't see that happening. She hates being married to me. She's only sticking with it while she gets her new modelling gig off the ground. She thinks marriage is an outdated institution that serves the interests of men rather than women.'

'Yes, well, it's certainly served your interests,' Raoul said.

'What's that supposed to mean?'

'You didn't have to sleep with her. You could have

got her out of Dharbiri and annulled the marriage once you got home.'

Remy flashed a glare his middle brother's way. 'Since when is who I sleep with your business?'

Raoul held his glare. 'If you divorce her, all hell could break loose. She could take half of your assets.'

'I thought you said she was a nice kid?'

'She is, but that's not to say she wouldn't want to get back at you for breaking her heart.'

'I'm not breaking her heart, OK?' Remy said in an exasperated tone. 'What is it with you and Rafe? You fall in love and expect everyone else to do the same. She doesn't even like me. I can't help thinking she's biding her time to turn things on their head. She's smart that way. She likes having the last word and she'll do anything to get it.'

'Have you really got so cynical you can't see what's right in front of your nose?'

'What? You think she loves me or something?' Remy said. 'Sorry to disappoint you, but Angelique's a great actress. She's no more in love with me than I am with her.'

Raoul gave him a look.

'What?' Remy gave another bark of a laugh but even to his ears it sounded hollow. 'You think *I'm* in love with *her*? Come on. No offence to you and Rafe, but falling in love is not on my list of things to do. I don't have that particular gene.'

'It's not a matter of genetics,' Raoul said. 'It's a matter of choice. If you're open to it, that is.'

'Well, I choose not to be open to it. I don't want that sort of complication in my life. I'm fine just the way I am.'

'You'll end up like *Nonno*,' Raoul said. 'Stuck with a

houseful of obsequious servants who pretend they like him when all they do is laugh and snigger about him behind his back.'

'I know what I'm doing, Raoul.'

'Yeah, and you're doing a damn fine job of it too. But, if you're so sure of Angelique's motives, why don't you give her Tarrantloch now and see if she still wants to stay with you? Take a gamble, Remy—or are you too scared of losing where it matters most?'

Remy let out a tight breath as his brother limped away to join Lily, who was looking at them with a worried frown.

Poppy came over with a cup of coffee and a slice cake for Remy. 'Have you seen Angelique?' she asked. 'She said she was going to the bathroom but she's been ages. Is she OK?'

'She's fine. She had a stomach bug a couple of days ago.' *How many times do I have to say this?* 'She's still getting over it.'

Poppy's expression flickered with something. 'Oh. I just wondered…'

'What?'

'Nothing.' She pinched her lips together as if afraid of speaking out of turn. She put a protective hand over her belly as a rosy blush spread over her cheeks.

Remy felt like someone had just slammed him in the solar plexus. It was a moment before he could get his breath back. His mind was reeling.

'Excuse me…' He almost pushed Poppy out of the way as he moved past.

CHAPTER FOURTEEN

ANGELIQUE LOOKED AT the dipstick.

Negative.

Why was she feeling so disappointed? It was ridiculous of her to feel so deflated. Why was she thinking about little dark-haired babies when she stood to gain squillions from parading around in bridal wear on every catwalk in Europe?

Because she didn't want to be a pretend bride.

Not on the catwalk. Not in a photo shoot. Not in magazines and billboards.

She wanted to be a real bride, a real wife and a real mother.

'Angelique?' There was a sharp rap at the door.

She quickly stuffed the packaging and results in the nearest drawer underneath the basin. ' Just a second…'

She checked her appearance in the mirror. She looked like she'd just auditioned for a walk-on part as a ghost in a horror movie.

The door handled rattled. 'Open this door,' Remy commanded. 'I want to talk to you.'

Angelique stalked over, snipped the lock back and opened the door. 'Do you mind? What does a girl have to do to get some privacy around here?'

He glanced to either side of her. 'What are you doing in there?'

She gave him a look. 'What do you think I was doing? What do you do when you go to the bathroom? No, on second thought, don't answer that.' She brushed past him. 'I know what you guys do.'

He captured her arm and turned her to face him. 'Are you pregnant?'

Angelique blinked at him in shock. 'What?'

His mouth was set in a grim line. 'I asked you a simple question. Are you pregnant?'

'No.'

'But you thought you were?'

She waited a beat before answering. 'Yes...'

He frowned so heavily his eyebrows met. 'And you didn't think to mention it to me?'

'I wanted to make sure first.'

'So you could do what? Announce it to the press? Post a tweet about it? Drop it on me to force me to keep our marriage going indefinitely?'

Angelique pushed past him. 'That's just so damn typical of you. You think everyone is going to do the dirty on you.'

'Do you realise how insulting this is?' He swung around to follow her. 'Don't you think I had the right to know you suspected you were carrying my child? This is something we should've been facing together. You had no right to keep that information to yourself.'

'You seem pretty certain it's your child,' Angelique said. ' How do you know I wasn't trying to foist another man's baby on you? You should watch your back, Remy. You think you're so smart, but I could have tricked you and you wouldn't have suspected a thing.'

'I don't believe you would sink to that level. You like

to act streetwise and tough but that's not who you really are. Your father might be a double-crossing cheat but you're not cut from the same cloth.'

'You don't know me.'

'I know you can't wait to get out of this marriage.' His jaw was locked tight with tension. 'Well, guess what? You got your wish. I'm releasing you. You're free to go as of now. I won't have anyone tell me I'm exploiting you by sleeping with you or getting you pregnant against your will, or keeping your precious castle just for kicks. Just go. Leave. Tarrantloch is yours. I'll send you the deeds.'

Angelique had dreamed of this moment, the moment when she would have Tarrantloch back in her possession. Why then did she feel like she was losing something even more valuable? 'You want me to leave?'

'That's what *you* want, isn't it?'

Here is your chance.

Tell him what you want.

But the words were stuck behind a wall of pride. What if she told him she loved him and wanted to stay with him for ever? He had never given any sign of being in love with her. Lust was his language. She had made it her own. If he loved her, wouldn't he have said so?

'Yes.' The word felt like a dry stone in her mouth. 'That's what I want.'

'Fine.' He let out a breath that sounded horribly, *distressingly* like relief. 'I won't make any announcements to the press until after Christmas. I don't want to compromise your modelling contract.'

That was the least of Angelique's worries. She was already trying to think of a way out of it. 'Thank you.' She pressed her lips together as she gathered up her bag.

She would not cry. She would not beg him to let her

stay. She would not tell him she loved him only to have him mock her. 'Will you say goodbye to the others for me? I don't want to create a scene.'

He gave a rough-sounding laugh. 'What? No big dramatic exit? You surprise me. That's not the Angelique Marchand I know.'

Angelique turned at the door and gave him a glacial look. 'Then perhaps you don't know me as well as you thought.'

As exit lines went, it was a good one. The only trouble was she could barely see where she was going for the tears that blurred her vision.

But she resolutely blinked them back and walked out of the villa and out of Remy's life without anyone stopping her.

And she wouldn't be coming back.

CHAPTER FIFTEEN

'But you can't possibly spend Christmas on your own!' Poppy said. 'Rafe, darling, will you tell your impossibly stubborn brother he's got to be with us? He won't listen to me.' Her bottom lip quivered as tears shimmered in her eyes. 'I can't bear the thought of anyone spending Christmas all alone.'

'It's nothing to get upset about,' Remy said, feeling like a heel for triggering Poppy's meltdown. 'I just don't feel like socialising, that's all.'

Rafe put his arm around Poppy and drew her close. 'Poppy's feeling a bit emotional just now, aren't you, *ma petite*?'

'I think we should tell him,' Poppy said with a little sniff.

'Tell me what?' Remy said, looking between the two of them.

'We're having a baby,' Rafe said with a proud smile. 'We found out a few weeks ago but didn't want to overshadow Raoul and Lily's wedding. We were going to wait until they got back from their honeymoon to announce it at Christmas.'

Remy's smile pulled on the tight ache in his chest that had been there since he had set Angelique free. 'Congratulations. I'm happy for you. That's great news.'

He even managed a short laugh. 'How about that? I'm going to be an uncle.'

'Will you *please* come to us for Christmas?' Poppy pleaded. 'I know you don't want to be anywhere near your grandfather just now, but we're supposed to be a family. It won't be the same without you there.'

It won't be the same without Angelique there.

Remy thought of the cosy family scene Poppy was so keen to orchestrate: wonderful cooking smells and warm fires in every room. A fresh pine-scented Christmas tree decorated with colourful bells and tinsel with thoughtfully chosen and artfully wrapped presents for everyone beneath it. His brothers and their wives would be talking non-stop about brides and honeymoons and babies. The photos from Raoul and Lily's wedding—where Angelique's absence in them would cause him even more pain—would be pored over and he would sit there being the odd one out—along with his grandfather, of course.

He'd rather be on his own than suffer that.

'Sorry, but I have other plans.'

'I wonder what Angelique has planned,' Poppy said as she handed back Rafe's handkerchief. 'Maybe I'll invite her. Do you think she'd come now that you're not going to be there?'

Remy frowned. 'Why would you invite her?'

'Why shouldn't I invite her?' Poppy gave him a haughty look. 'I loved her the minute I met her. So did Lily.'

'You spent all of five minutes with her!'

'Maybe, but it was enough to know she's a lovely person.'

'I never said she wasn't.' Remy caught his brother's look. 'Lately, I mean.'

'Did you know she's cancelled the bridal wear contract?' Rafe said. 'It will cost her a fortune to get out of. One of the designers is threatening to sue.'

Remy felt his stomach drop. 'Where did you hear that?'

'Social media,' Rafe said. 'Where else?'

Angelique stood back and inspected the tree she had set up in the sitting room of Tarrantloch. The scent of pine filled the air with a pleasantly sharp, clean tang. It brought back wonderful memories of Christmas with her grandparents all those years ago. She had even found in the attic the decorations they had used back then—miraculously overlooked by the ruthlessly efficient removal men—including the angel she had loved so much as a child. The angel was looking a little the worse for wear with her yellowed robes and moth-eaten wings but Angelique didn't have the heart to replace her.

The festive season was the worst time to be alone. She had spent far too many of them in hotel rooms or with people she didn't particularly know or like to do it again this year.

Poppy had invited her to spend it with her and Rafe in Oxfordshire, with Lily, Raoul and Vittorio, but she'd politely declined, even when Poppy had assured her Remy wasn't going to be there. Angelique hadn't asked where he would be spending Christmas or who he'd be spending it with.

She didn't want to know.

The sound of helicopter blades outside gave her a little start. Robert Mappleton wasn't due to arrive until tomorrow, on Christmas Eve. She had invited him because she'd found out he had spent every Christmas alone since his wife had died.

Angelique peered out of the window, but it wasn't Robert who got out of the helicopter. Her heart banged against her chest as Remy came through the icy wind towards the house. She dusted off the tinsel sparkles clinging to her yoga pants before opening the front door. 'What are you doing here?'

'I want to talk to you.'

She folded her arms. 'So talk.'

'Aren't you going to invite me in?'

She put her chin up. 'I'm expecting company.'

He flinched as if she'd just struck him. 'Who?'

Angelique saw his throat move up and down. His eyes looked tired. He needed a shave more than usual. 'Robert Mappleton.'

His expression turned to stone. Unreadable stone. 'I guess I should've guessed that.'

Angelique unfolded her arms. 'Why aren't you spending Christmas with your family?'

He gave her a brooding look. 'I don't trust myself in the same room as my grandfather. Every time I see him I want to punch him.'

'I told my father I *would* punch him if he came anywhere near me.'

Remy stood looking at her for a beat of silence. 'So…I guess I should leave you to it…' He raked a hand through his windblown hair. He was too late. He'd left it too late. His gamble hadn't paid off. She had moved on with her life. Robert Mappleton was far too old for her but she was probably searching for a father figure, given hers was so appalling.

He was too late.

'Why are you here?' Angelique asked.

Remy was sick of all the game playing, the pretence

and subterfuge. He decided to take one last gamble. His pride was on the table but it was a small price to pay.

It was the price he was prepared to pay.

'I wanted to tell you I love you.'

Her eyelids flickered. 'You...*love* me?'

Remy gave her a self-deprecating look. 'You looked shocked.'

'But you never said a word... You sent me away.' She narrowed her gaze at him, her cheeks firing up with red-hot anger. 'How could you *do* that to me?'

Remy took umbrage at her cutting tone. 'I thought that's what you wanted. For God's sake, I asked you straight out what you wanted. You said you only wanted Tarrantloch.'

'I was pretending!' Angelique said. 'How could you think I would want a big old, draughty castle instead of love?'

Now it was his turn to look shocked. 'You want love?'

Angelique felt tears prickling at the back of her throat. 'I want love and marriage and...and a baby.'

Remy blinked. 'You want a baby?'

She brushed at her eyes with the back of her hand. 'I know you're going to think this is utterly ridiculous, but I was bitterly disappointed when that pregnancy test was negative.'

'Why?'

'Because without it I had no reason to stay with you.'

'But what about your modelling contract?'

'You just don't get it, do you?' Angelique said. 'You don't get me at all. I *hate* being a model. I hate having to look perfect all the time. I only ever got into it because I knew it would annoy my father. I want to design clothes, not parade around in them.'

Remy took her by the shoulders. 'You want to stay with me? Is that what you're saying?'

Angelique looked up into his dark brown eyes. 'I've wanted to stay with you since the night you put on *The Lion King* when I was fifteen and watched it with me.'

Remy's fingers tightened. He was frightened to let go of her in case this was all a dream. 'You love me?'

'Desperately.'

'Then why the hell didn't you say so?' He glared at her. 'Do you realise the torture you've put me through? I could put you over my knee and spank you.'

Angelique gave him a cheeky smile. 'Is that a promise?'

He clutched her to his chest, almost crushing her in the process. 'I thought I'd lost you. I thought it was too late. I thought *I* was too late. When Rafe told me he'd heard a rumour you were trying to get out of your contract I started to think...*to hope*...it was because you weren't happy with your life.' He pulled back to look at her. 'Tell me I'm not dreaming this.'

She smoothed away the frown between his brows with her fingertip. 'Do you think we're always going to fight?'

He captured her finger and kissed its tip. 'I hope so. It's so much fun making up.'

Angelique's eyes sparkled. 'Do you think Robert Mappleton would mind if we have a slight change of venue for Christmas?'

'What did you have in mind?'

She toyed with his shirt collar. 'Well...it sounds like Poppy's gone to a lot of trouble and it would be really nice to have a proper family Christmas for once. And I really want to see Raoul and Lily's wedding photos and hear all about their honeymoon.' She lifted her gaze to his. 'Would you mind?'

'For you, *mon amour*, I would agree to anything. But first I have something to give you.' He took out a box from his anorak pocket and handed it to her.

Angelique opened the box to find an engagement and wedding ring ensemble that was so exquisitely and yet so simply crafted it took her breath away. She blinked away a sudden rush of tears and looked up into his gaze. 'It's perfect! It's absolutely gorgeous! How did you know I would love this so much?'

He gave her a twinkling smile as he scooped her up into his arms. 'I took a gamble.'

EPILOGUE

REMY LOOKED AROUND the sitting room of Dalrymple House where his family was gathered for Christmas. His grandfather was sitting grumbling about the stock market fluctuations with a very patient Robert Mappleton. Raoul was sitting on the sofa with his legs up on an ottoman. Lily was tucked in close to his side, looking up at him with such rapt attention it made Remy's chest feel warm. Rafe was helping Poppy carry in egg nog and nibbles but stopped in the doorway to give her a lingering kiss under the mistletoe.

Remy looked across at Angelique who was on the floor in front of the Christmas tree cuddling all three of Poppy's cute little dogs. Chutney, Pickles and Relish were instantly besotted with her and had no shame about showing it. Pickles—who according to Rafe was a hard nut to crack—had even snuck in an extra couple of licks.

Angelique laughed as she got off the floor to come over to Remy. 'Did you see that, darling? I won Pickles over straight away. He couldn't resist me.'

'I saw you sneak him a treat,' Remy said. 'In my book, that's cheating.'

She gave him a grin as she wound her arms around

his middle. 'You're just jealous because you didn't think of it first.'

'I'm not jealous.'

'Yes you are.'

'Am not.'

'Will someone tell those two to stop bickering?' Rafe said from over by the mistletoe.

'They're not bickering,' Raoul said from the sofa. 'They're just warming up for a kiss. See, what did I tell you? Any second now. *Bingo*.'

* * * * *

A sneaky peek at next month...

MODERN™

INTERNATIONAL AFFAIRS, SEDUCTION & PASSION GUARANTEED

My wish list for next month's titles...

In stores from 15th November 2013:

- ❏ Defiant in the Desert – Sharon Kendrick
- ❏ Rumours on the Red Carpet – Carole Mortimer
- ❏ His Ultimate Prize – Maya Blake
- ❏ More than a Convenient Marriage? – Dani Collins

In stores from 6th December 2013:

- ❏ Not Just the Boss's Plaything – Caitlin Crews
- ❏ The Change in Di Navarra's Plan – Lynn Raye Harris
- ❏ The Prince She Never Knew – Kate Hewitt
- ❏ A Golden Betrayal – Barbara Dunlop

Available at WHSmith, Tesco, Asda, Eason, Amazon and Apple

Just can't wait?

1113/01

Special Offers

Every month we put together collections and longer reads written by your favourite authors.

Here are some of next month's highlights— and don't miss our fabulous discount online!

On sale 6th December

On sale 1st November

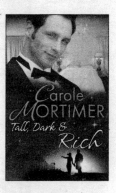

On sale 6th December

Save 20%
on all Special Releases

Come home this Christmas to Fiona Harper

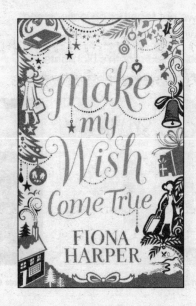

Make my Wish Come True

FIONA HARPER

From the author of *Kiss Me Under the Mistletoe* comes a Christmas tale of family and fun. Two sisters are ready to swap their Christmases—the busy super-mum, Juliet, getting the chance to escape it all on an exotic Christmas getaway, whilst her glamorous work-obsessed sister, Gemma, is plunged headfirst into the family Christmas she always thought she'd hate.

www.millsandboon.co.uk

1113/MB442

Wrap up warm this winter with Sarah Morgan...

Sleigh Bells in the Snow

Kayla Green loves business and hates Christmas.

So when Jackson O'Neil invites her to Snow Crystal Resort to discuss their business proposal... the last thing she's expecting is to stay for Christmas dinner. As the snowflakes continue to fall, will the woman who doesn't believe in the magic of Christmas finally fall under its spell...?

4th October

www.millsandboon.co.uk/sarahmorgan

3/MB435